# A Perilous P

Nancy gazed in awe as a liveried butler opened the door to the Van Hoogstraten mansion, where Delphinia Van Hoogstraten was hosting a dinner dance. The butler ushered Nancy, her aunt Eloise, George, and Bess into a huge marble foyer with an enormous crystal chandelier.

"Eloise!" a woman's voice cried out through the crowd of guests. "How wonderful to see you." The woman, who was wearing a gold silk dress, glided over to them.

"Dell!" Aunt Eloise said, embracing her friend. "Please meet my niece, Nancy Drew, and her friends, Bess Marvin and George Fayne."

Before anyone could say another word, a creaking noise erupted from above them. Nancy looked up and gasped. The huge chandelier in the center of the ceiling was dangling on a broken chain.

Before she could alert Dell, the chain suddenly broke. The chandelier, like a giant spider poised to embrace them with sharp deadly legs, plunged toward them.

# Nancy Drew
# Mystery Stories

#104 The Mystery of the Jade Tiger
#108 The Secret of the Tibetan Treasure
#110 The Nutcracker Ballet Mystery
#112 Crime in the Queen's Court
#116 The Case of the Twin Teddy Bears
#117 Mystery on the Menu
#119 The Mystery of the Missing Mascot
#120 The Case of the Floating Crime
#123 The Clue on the Silver Screen
#125 The Teen Model Mystery
#126 The Riddle in the Rare Book
#127 The Case of the Dangerous Solution
#128 The Treasure in the Royal Tower
#129 The Baby-sitter Burglaries
#130 The Sign of the Falcon
#132 The Fox Hunt Mystery
#133 The Mystery at the Crystal Palace
#134 The Secret of the Forgotten Cave
#135 The Riddle of the Ruby Gazelle
#136 The Wedding Day Mystery
#137 In Search of the Black Rose
#138 The Legend of the Lost Gold
#139 The Secret of Candlelight Inn

#140 The Door-to-Door Deception
#141 The Wild Cat Crime
#142 The Case of Capital Intrigue
#143 Mystery on Maui
#144 The E-mail Mystery
#145 The Missing Horse Mystery
#146 The Ghost of the Lantern Lady
#147 The Case of the Captured Queen
#148 On the Trail of Trouble
#149 The Clue of the Gold Doubloons
#150 Mystery at Moorsea Manor
#151 The Chocolate-Covered Contest
#152 The Key in the Satin Pocket
#153 Whispers in the Fog
#154 The Legend of the Emerald Lady
#155 The Mystery in Tornado Alley
#156 The Secret in the Stars
#157 The Music Festival Mystery
#158 The Curse of the Black Cat
#159 The Secret of the Fiery Chamber
#160 The Clue on the Crystal Dove
Nancy Drew Ghost Stories

## Available from MINSTREL Books

# NANCY DREW® 160

## THE CLUE ON THE CRYSTAL DOVE

CAROLYN KEENE

A MINSTREL® BOOK

Published by POCKET BOOKS
New York  London  Toronto  Sydney  Singapore

This book is a work of fiction. Names, characters, places and incidents are products of the author's imagination or are used fictitiously. Any resemblance to actual events or locales or persons living or dead is entirely coincidental.

A MINSTREL PAPERBACK *Original*

A Minstrel Book published by
POCKET BOOKS, a division of Simon & Schuster, Inc.
1230 Avenue of the Americas, New York, NY 10020

ISBN: 0-7434-0686-9

First Minstrel Books printing June 2001

10  9  8  7  6  5  4  3  2  1

Front cover illustration by Frank Sofo

Printed in the U.S.A.

# Contents

1   *Total Darkness*    1

2   *A Secret Compartment*    12

3   *Mystery Lady*    22

4   *Disaster before Dinner*    28

5   *A Wild Accusation*    39

6   *Sneak Thief*    47

7   *Skeleton with a Message*    57

8   *A Terrifying Call*    65

9   *Danger on the Bridge*    74

10   *Surprise at the Door*    86

11   *Crazy Horse*    97

12   *Clued In*    108

13   *A Ghostly Welcome*    116

14   *Terror on the Lake*    127

15   *Birds of a Feather*    136

# THE CLUE ON THE
# CRYSTAL DOVE

# 1

## Total Darkness

"All aboard!" the train conductor shouted. "Chicago to New York City—and all stops in between!"

Nancy Drew and her father, Carson, stepped up their pace as Carson pushed a trolley laden with luggage along the crowded platform of the cavernous station. Nancy's best friends, George Fayne and Bess Marvin, hurried to keep up.

"Will we make it?" Bess asked Nancy as the train whistle shrilled through the humid air.

"I think so, Bess," Nancy said, "though I can't predict whether all four of your suitcases will get on before the doors close."

"Don't say that!" Bess moaned. "I need them.

We'll be in New York a whole week, and the party that Delphinia's planning sounds awesome."

"This is all I brought," George declared as she stepped up to her friends. She patted the straps of a large backpack slung over her shoulders.

"Don't tell me your dress for Delphinia's big dinner event is crumpled up in there," Bess said, looking horrified.

"Not crumpled—rolled," George countered. "It's made out of some nonwrinkling material—ideal for travel-by-backpack," she quipped, in the tone of a commercial. "Though I probably should have packed an extra pair of sneakers for sightseeing."

"Sightseeing? As in checking out cool shops and restaurants?" Bess asked mischievously.

"No way. Sightseeing, as in visiting the Museum of Natural History and hiking across the Brooklyn Bridge," George retorted with a toss of her short dark hair.

Bess made a face. "Sounds like torture. All the sights I'm interested in seeing can be found in Bloomingdale's. And you don't need sneakers for that."

Eighteen-year-old Nancy grinned at her friends' remarks. Bess and George were first cousins and devoted friends, but they were also total opposites. Blond-haired Bess loved clothes, high-calorie desserts, and boy watching, while George's interests ran more to athletics. Nancy knew that planning activities in the Big Apple to interest both girls would be complicated.

"Is this a sleeping car?" Nancy's father asked a conductor standing next to a car with high, wide windows.

"Indeed it is," the conductor declared. "May I see your tickets, please?"

"I've got them, Dad," Nancy said, reaching into her purse. She handed three tickets to the conductor.

"Miss Drew, Miss Fayne, and Miss Marvin," the conductor said as he examined the tickets. "You've come to the right car, ladies. Compartment Twenty-three B. Step lively, please. The train leaves in exactly three minutes."

"Why don't I help you girls load this stuff into your compartment?" Carson offered, sweeping suitcases from the trolley onto the metal platform inside the car door. "I can do that in less than three minutes."

"Just keep an ear out for the conductor's last call, Dad," Nancy warned, "unless you want a surprise trip to New York."

Carson chuckled. "If I didn't have to be in court tomorrow in River Heights, a trip to New York would be great," he said, hefting three suitcases. "I could tour the Empire State Building, the Statue of Liberty, the Metropolitan Museum of Art—the list is endless. New York is like one gigantic grab bag full of things to do."

"Not to mention visiting Delphinia Van Hoog-

3

straten's mansion with its famous collection of glass birds," Nancy reminded him. "Here, Dad, let me give you a hand with the bags." She hoisted two suitcases, followed her father down the narrow aisle of the sleeping car, and stopped outside the door marked 23B.

Sliding it open, she found two blue velour sofas facing each other with a window in the wall beside them. Large cabinets ran the length of the walls over the sofas.

"The conductor will convert one of these sofas into a bed later on," Carson explained as he entered the compartment behind Nancy. "Those overhead cabinets will open to make two more beds."

"There's room for the luggage under the sofas," Nancy commented, pushing her suitcase under the sofa on her right.

"Last call!" the conductor shouted into the car. "All those without tickets please exit immediately."

"Goodbye, girls, and take good care of Eloise," Carson said, referring to his sister, who lived in New York. "I'm glad you'll be staying with her instead of at some hotel. And, Nancy—try not to get involved in a mystery," he added with a wink. "Every good professional needs time off, and detectives are no exception."

"I'll try my best, Dad," Nancy promised, smiling. After giving her father a hug, she watched him hurry down the aisle and off the train. The instant he stepped on to the platform, the conductor slammed the car door shut, and the train inched forward.

"I agree with your dad—no mysteries!" Bess exclaimed. "I have this feeling that just bringing up the subject will jinx us. With your track record, Nan, there's sure to be a mystery lurking somewhere on this train."

George propped her backpack in a niche by the door and said, "I hope not. Your dad's right, Nancy. Even ace detectives need time off."

"And I plan to take it," Nancy said firmly, settling herself on a sofa and peering out the window as the train slid into a tunnel. "Our week in New York will be total vacation, I promise. We'll explore the city, see Aunt Eloise, and meet her friend Delphinia Van Hoogstraten—Dell for short."

"Tell me more about Dell," Bess said as she and George sat down on the sofa across from Nancy. "Why is she turning her mansion into a museum?"

As the train rattled out of the tunnel and into the sunshine, Nancy thought back to her conversation with her aunt Eloise about the eccentric Van Hoogstraten family. She'd told Bess and George only a few details about them.

"According to Aunt Eloise," Nancy explained, "Dell's getting married and moving to Boston, where her fiancé lives. The mansion is owned by a Van

Hoogstraten family partnership, and they've decided to turn it into a museum."

George's dark eyes narrowed thoughtfully. "But if a bunch of Van Hoogstratens own the mansion, how come Dell ended up living in it by herself?"

"Dell's an only child, and she grew up in the house, so the place means a lot to her," Nancy replied as she looked out the window. Green fields and leafy trees flashed by like a movie on fast-forward. Turning her eyes from the afternoon sunlight that flooded into the compartment, she added, "I think Dell pays rent to the partnership. For some reason, none of Julius's other descendants is interested in living there."

"Julius?" Bess cut in. "Who's he?"

"Dell's great-grandfather Julius Van Hoogstraten, who built the house," Nancy replied. "He died in 1915."

"The Van Hoogstratens must be mega rich in order to afford the taxes and upkeep on a huge place like that in New York City," George commented.

"You said it, George," Nancy declared. "Julius Van Hoogstraten was one of the richest men in New York during the Gilded Age. He made this unbelievable fortune in railroads."

"The Gilded Age?" Bess echoed, puzzled.

Pulling her reddish blond hair into a quick ponytail, Nancy explained, "That's a nickname for the late 1800s when all these people became millionaires.

They lived incredibly fancy lives—people like Cornelius Vanderbilt, J. P. Morgan, and John D. Rockefeller, who made money from shipping and banking and oil. They built these huge mansions and had tons of servants."

"Those guys must have really raked in the dough," George commented, "especially because they didn't have income taxes in those days."

"The amount of money they had was mind-boggling," Nancy went on, "and they loved to flaunt it. Balls and dinner parties for hundreds of guests, humongous summer homes, and honeymoons around the world were typical."

"But what's so special about Julius's mansion? Why would it rate as a museum?" George asked. "Did he have a big art collection or something?"

"Julius had this awesome collection of blown-glass birds," Nancy told her. "He'd made them himself in Holland before moving to America, when he was twenty-five. They were so beautiful that he couldn't stand the thought of leaving them behind. Now his collection is priceless."

"Who would have thought that a talent for making glass birds would have led him to a fortune in railroads?" Bess remarked.

"Aunt Eloise said that he came to America with his glass bird collection and a few pennies in his pocket," Nancy went on, kicking off her shoes and folding her legs under herself. "He started working as a train mechanic, saved money, and when an opportunity came to buy a struggling railroad, he seized it. But apparently his newfound money went to his head. He threw fancy parties—even for his pets' birthdays—smoked cigars and drank expensive brandy, and was known for being bossy and rude. He fired servants right and left, except for his pastry chef, who could do no wrong."

Bess perked up. "Hmm. I wonder if the chef left any of his recipes somewhere in the house—maybe in old letters or cookbooks? That's the kind of mystery I'd be up for solving, Nan. Nothing dangerous—but with a definite payoff."

"Speaking of food," George said, checking her watch, "it's five o'clock. Why don't we explore the train before dinner?"

Nancy's blue eyes sparkled excitedly. "I forgot to tell you guys—Julius's private railroad car has been totally restored. It's attached to this train, and we can tour it."

"What a coincidence!" Bess exclaimed.

"Not exactly," Nancy admitted. "The Van Hoogstratens arranged to have it attached to certain routes in the Northeast to promote the opening of their musuem. So when I called to make our reservations, I learned that the car would be on this particular train. That's why we're traveling today."

The girls stepped out of their compartment and headed down the corridor toward the rear of the train. The next car they entered was the dining car. Nancy was surprised to see how crowded it was already. People were sitting at tables covered with white cloths and set with gleaming cutlery. Most of the diners were studying menus while white-coated waiters looked on attentively, ready with pads to take orders.

The maître d' approached the girls. "Would you like to have a table, ladies?" he asked in a friendly manner. "A couple of tables are still available."

"Not yet, thanks," Nancy said with a polite smile. "We thought we'd explore the Julius Van Hoogstraten car first."

"Well, you're in luck," the maître d' said. "A gentleman from the Van Hoogstraten mansion is giving tours of the car starting at eight o'clock. He's suggesting to people that they wait for his tour so they can learn interesting details about Van Hoogstraten's life and times."

"We don't need a formal tour," Nancy began when the train gave a sudden lurch. Nancy, George, and Bess fell backward a step, colliding with an empty booth.

Before Nancy could say another word, the lights in the car flickered and then suddenly went out. Nothing, not even a shadow, was visible.

Bess screamed as diners let out exclamations of

surprise. The sound of dishes breaking clattered from the kitchen.

"Huh?" Nancy heard a woman say.

A screeching sound filled the air as the train slowed. Nancy heard Bess gasp as it stopped.

"We just entered a tunnel, that's why it's so dark," the maître d' said.

"I can't see a thing," George said. "But I can feel a booth here. Let's sit down, guys. Are you near me?"

"Yes," Nancy and Bess said together. After feeling for the seats, they sat down with George.

"All the power is off," the maître d' remarked. "No air conditioner, no stove, no nothing."

"It's getting so hot," Bess said. "I can hardly breathe. And this car is kind of crowded."

"Don't worry, Bess," George said. "I hear a conductor coming. I'm sure he'll take care of the problem."

"If only we hadn't stopped inside a tunnel," Bess said weakly. "I'm getting claustrophobic."

Nancy saw a flashlight bob down the aisle. A set of keys rattled behind the light in the darkness.

"Hey, Fred!" the conductor shouted. "Are you getting a connection?"

"Not yet." Fred's frustrated voice sounded from the front of the car. "I'm going to the engine."

The conductor with his light bustled out as the temperature in the car rose.

10

Perspiration formed on Nancy's face. The car *was* hot, she thought.

"What's that smell?" Bess asked, sounding panicked.

"What smell?" George said.

"Smoke!" Bess replied.

"Bess, relax," Nancy said soothingly.

Even Nancy couldn't ignore the smell of smoke that suddenly gusted into the already hot and stuffy air. What is going on? she wondered.

A woman's cry broke through the silence from a table behind them. "Fire!"

# 2

## A Secret Compartment

"Hush!" Nancy heard the maître d' say in a low voice. "I assure you, ma'am, you're wrong."

"Let's get out of here, guys!" Bess urged, ignoring the maître d's calming words. "The smoke is getting thicker."

"Wait, Bess," Nancy said. "Don't bolt. People will hear you and panic. We'll have a stampede."

Nancy sniffed the air. The smoke had an oddly familiar spicy scent—not like a fire at all, she thought.

"What's that over there—glowing in the dark?" George asked, gripping Nancy's arm.

Now two feet away from Nancy, a gleam of light looked like tiny coals bobbing across a pitch-black screen.

The light zoomed a foot to the right as a man's cough rumbled through the silence.

"It's only a pipe!" Nancy exclaimed.

"What? I'm such an idiot," Bess said, with a giggle of relief.

"The man who's smoking it must be walking down the aisle," George remarked.

"Sir, sir!" said the woman who'd cried "fire." Her voice resonated from the booth behind them as she tried to get the smoker's attention. "Sir, this train is strictly no-smoking. Please have the courtesy to put out your pipe."

"I'm so sorry." The man's gruff voice cut through the darkness, which seemed to envelop everyone like a stiflingly hot blanket. "I always smoke when I'm nervous," he continued apologetically.

Several taps sounded from nearby, and Nancy guessed the man was extinguishing his pipe. "There, that's done," he said.

"Even if there is no fire," Bess said quietly, "we're still stuck here in the dark. And the air is really hot. How long do you guys think oxygen lasts in a situation like this?"

"Don't worry, Bess," Nancy said, placing a comforting arm around her friend's shoulder. "The train crew will fix the problem, or if worse comes to worst, they'll evacuate the train through the tunnel. But I doubt it will come to that. In any case, we definitely won't suffocate."

Bess took a deep breath. "Thanks for the reassurance, Nan. I mean, I wouldn't want to miss out on wearing my hot new dress to Dell's party," she added wryly.

After a tense ten minutes, light flooded back into the car. The passengers jumped in their seats, some closing their eyes from the sudden brightness. Nancy, George, and Bess blinked at one another in surprise, then squinted to see what was happening.

A door opened at the far end of the car, and two conductors hurried through it. An anxious silence fell over the passengers as they waited to hear what the train officials would say.

"Please don't worry, ladies and gentlemen," the first conductor called out. "Some circuit breakers tripped, but we've fixed 'em and now this train is back in the running." As if to illustrate his words, the train began to lurch forward.

"We're running a half hour behind schedule," the second conductor announced, "but we'll try to make it up by putting on a little extra steam."

The moment the conductors moved into the next car, the dining car erupted into mixed comments of relief and annoyance.

"Thanks heavens the problem was only a circuit

breaker, and we'll only be a half hour late," said a woman.

"Don't believe it for a moment," said the pipe smoker. "They're just feeding us a line so we won't panic—or sue."

"Well, ladies," the maître d' said, approaching Nancy, Bess, and George. "What do you say to some dinner? You must be starving after our little adventure. Why don't I send over a waiter to take your order?"

Bess smiled at him as she took a menu. "Thanks There's nothing more soothing than a good dinner and a piece of chocolate cake to finish it off," she said brightly.

"Aha! I will reserve a piece of our double chocolate walnut cake especially for you," the maître d' promised.

The door to the dining car was suddenly opened. A tall brown-haired young man with light hazel eyes stepped through it and approached the maître d'. Dressed in a white tie, black tails, and a top hat, he looked both elegant and strange.

"I can't figure out whether he looks handsome or dorky," Bess whispered to Nancy and George. "I mean, why is he dressed up like that just to have dinner on a train?"

"He looks like one of those symphony orchestra musicians," George said, staring at him as if he were a creature from another planet.

"Or like an ad for men's clothes from a hundred years ago," Nancy remarked.

Before they could say another word, the man and the maître d' approached them.

"I would like to introduce Mr. Alden Guest," the maître d' said. "He's the gentleman I mentioned who gives tours of the Van Hoogstraten railway car. Since the rest of my dining car is full, would you mind if Mr. Guest dines with you? He has to eat now because later he'll be conducting tours."

"Have a seat," Nancy said, smiling at Alden as she made room for him on her side of the table.

The girls introduced themselves, and then the waiter took everyone's order.

"We were wondering why you're dressed like that," George said to Alden after the maître d' had left. "Is it because you're a tour guide?"

Alden grinned, showing a set of brilliant white teeth. "You guessed correctly, George. I'm really a New York banker, but I've volunteered some vacation time over the next couple of weeks to publicize the opening of the Van Hoogstraten museum. Right now I'm in charge of the Van Hoogstraten railroad car. It's been attached to certain trains to promote the museum, which opens in five days."

"Wow!" Bess said. "So Dell is moving out of her house in five days?"

The expression on Alden's handsome face was one

16

of surprise. "Dell?" he said. "How do you know my cousin Dell?"

Nancy quickly explained about her aunt Eloise's friendship with Delphinia Van Hoogstraten. "Aunt Eloise also told me about Dell's great-grandfather's mansion and his collection of glass birds," she finished.

"Julius Van Hoogstraten was my great-grandfather, too," Alden said. "Dell's father and my mother were brother and sister, though many years apart in age. Dell is in her early forties, while I'm twenty years younger."

Bess smiled shyly at Alden. "It's too bad that you have to slave away all evening giving people tours of your great-grandfather's car. Otherwise you could have hung out with us."

"Some other time," Alden promised, fixing Bess with a dazzling smile. "But why don't I take you on your own personal tour of the car before I get busy with the tour groups at eight? We've got plenty of time—it's only six now."

"That would be great," Bess gushed, and Nancy and George nodded in agreement.

The waiter brought their dinners, along with their soft drinks. As Nancy dug into her lasagna, Alden turned to the girls and asked, "How long are you going to be in New York?"

"A week," Nancy said. "We'll be able to see the

museum after it opens. But if Dell invites us to see it earlier, we'll jump at the chance."

"You don't need her to invite you," Alden said dismissively. "I'd be happy to let you into the museum any time. And by the way, how much has your aunt told you about Julius's collection?"

"Not a whole lot," Nancy said. "Just that he kept his glass birds in a room that looks like a greenhouse."

Alden nodded. "Julius called it the aviary, and he divided it into a bunch of different regions of the world, like a tropical rain forest or a northern wood. He gave each bird its own habitat using silk trees and flowers."

"It sounds really cool," Bess said, her blue eyes shining. "How did Julius get to be so talented? It's amazing that a rich businessman would also be an artist type."

"Julius loved ornithology, which is the study of birds," Alden replied. "After he became rich, he would travel all over the world to exotic places to birdwatch. He'd record each new species he saw in his diary. Some of his rich friends only cared about money, but birdwatching was Julius's passion."

"How did he learn to blow glass?" George asked. "That sounds like a really hard skill."

"When my great-grandfather was a young man in Holland, he served as an apprentice to a famous glassblower named Gustav Kinderhook," Alden said, spearing a piece of lettuce with his fork. "He learned his craft from Gustav. But after Julius brought his birds to America, he no longer had time to make new ones. He had to be satisfied with displaying the ones he'd already made in Holland."

"He must have been so proud of them," Bess said.

Alden finished his salad and said, "He was extremely proud of them—more than he was of his huge railroad empire. In one of his letters, he said that anyone could get rich with a little luck and hard work, but very few people can be artists, no matter how hard they try."

"So was he famous for his collection when he was alive?" Nancy asked.

"He didn't allow the public to see it," Alden answered. "After all, he kept the birds in his private house. But the few glass experts who saw his collection considered it to be extraordinary. They wrote books on the subject and raved about the Van Hoogstraten Collection—which is what we're calling our museum."

After dessert was served, Bess asked, "How do you have time to know about banking and glass birds? You must be a chip off the old block. I mean, you're exactly like Julius—multitalented."

"Give me a break, Bess," George said, rolling her eyes. "Or rather, give poor Alden a break."

"No, it's okay," Alden said, squaring his shoulders

proudly. "I'm flattered to be compared to my great-grandfather. Of course, I don't deserve it."

"Now you're fishing," Bess teased, pushing aside the remains of her chocolate cake. "But speaking of your great-grandfather, why don't you show us his railway coach? I'm dying to see for myself how he lived."

After signing their checks, Alden, Bess, George, and Nancy headed for the end of the train. They passed through another sleeping car before walking inside Julius's coach—the last car on the train.

Nancy looked around, awestruck. She felt as if she had entered another world. The mahogany paneling of the walls was a rich burnished red-brown. The maroon velvet upholstery on the sofa and armchairs looked as soft as a cat's fur. The crystal chandelier and wall sconces imparted a golden glow. And the framed sepia photographs of Victorian men and women adorning the walls spoke hauntingly of people who had lived long ago.

Nancy traded glances with Bess and George. She could tell they all agreed that Julius's coach was a sight to behold.

"I thought our train compartment was pretty cushy," George said, shooting a grin at Alden. "But now you've totally spoiled me."

"It is incredible, isn't it?" Alden said. "Look at this." He pulled a wooden handle that stuck out of a nearby wall, and a bed eased itself down on top of the sofa. With its antique wooden headboard, puffy mattress, and lace bedspread, it reminded Nancy of an illustration she'd once seen of the bed in "The Princess and the Pea."

"Look at this headboard," Nancy breathed, fingering the carved wood. Eight squares, each filled with a different kind of carved bird, decorated it.

"Try it out," Alden offered, gesturing grandly at the bed. "The mattress is made of pure goosedown—awesomely comfortable."

"Is this guy Julius?" Bess broke in from across the room. As Alden and George moved to a portrait in the opposite corner, Nancy sank down on the bed. Without meaning to touch the headboard, she tapped her head lightly against one of the middle squares.

Was she dreaming—or was the square giving way? Maybe the wood is rotten, she thought, as she straightened up and turned around to look.

Nancy blinked. The square was sliding open!

# 3

## Mystery Lady

"Look, guys!" Nancy exclaimed. "A secret compartment."

Peering inside, Nancy saw some yellowing envelopes. Addresses had been scrawled on them in ink, now faded with age. Old letters, she concluded—probably Julius's.

Bess, George, and Alden moved quickly to her side. Reaching over her head, Alden shut the panel.

"Very interesting, Nancy," he pronounced. "I'll have to check that out later. Now, where was I? Talking about Julius, I think."

As he returned to the portrait with Bess and George, Nancy thought about his response to her discovery. He doesn't seem surprised by the panel, she thought. Maybe he already knows about it.

Nancy stole a look behind her. Alden, Bess, and George were busy studying a portrait of a gray-haired man in his sixties with an aquiline nose, steely blue eyes, and a stern expression. Bushy mutton-chop whiskers on the sides of his cheeks and a starched collar marked him as being from a totally different era. On the tip of his forefinger perched a crystal dove.

He must be Julius, Nancy reasoned. But despite his grim expression and old-fashioned hair, Nancy could tell that Julius must have been quite handsome in his youth, with his strong jaw, piercing eyes, and chiseled features.

She glanced back at the secret panel, feeling suddenly intrigued by Julius's Gilded Age world. It would take only a few seconds to skim through one of the letters, she thought, but Alden had clearly put them off limits.

Fighting her curiosity, Nancy memorized which bird decorated the secret panel—an eagle, she observed.

Climbing off the bed, Nancy walked over to join Bess and George as Alden pointed out a print of the Van Hoogstraten mansion in New York. But her thoughts were wandering far from what he was saying.

Maybe I'll sneak back here later tonight and take a look at those letters when no one's around, Nancy mused, her mind clicking away as Alden spoke. Julius seems like such a complicated guy, she thought. From everything Alden had said and from what she knew of his life, Julius was a tough businessman as well as a sensitive artist. How could such opposite types exist in one person? she wondered.

Even though he'd been dead for several generations, Nancy couldn't help but be curious about such a contradictory and powerful character. In trying to figure out Julius, she almost felt as if she had stumbled across a type of mystery.

Nancy glanced again at the portrait. She could easily trace the Gilded Age tycoon in Julius's haughty features, but nowhere in his bold face could she detect any hint of the nature-loving artist.

There's only one real way to get a sense of this guy, she concluded—by studying his letters and diaries.

Alden's gaze suddenly flew to his watch. "It's almost eight," he announced. "I'm due to give a tour now. I'd much rather hang out with you guys, of course, but you're welcome to stay while the tour comes in."

"Thanks, Alden," Nancy said, "but I'm pretty tired. Maybe Bess and George will take you up on your offer."

Bess stifled a yawn. "I'd love to stay, but you gave us such a great private tour, Alden, that it wouldn't be the same with a crowd."

"Exactly my thoughts," George said. "Thank you

so much, Alden. Will we see you at Dell's dinner party tomorrow night?"

Alden flashed his brilliant smile. "You can count on it. But only if all three of you promise to dance at least once with me."

Nancy gave him the thumbs-up sign. Then they all thanked him again and moved toward the car door while an elderly couple, two young women, and the man with the pipe streamed into the car. Once the girls reached their compartment, they found the beds pulled down for them.

"Perfect!" Bess said. "I can get my beauty sleep before hitting the dance floor at Dell's tomorrow night."

Nancy curled up on her bed with a book. "You know what, guys?" she said. "I'd love to read those letters in the secret compartment. I'm really curious to know more about Julius."

"But what if Alden catches you?" Bess asked. "While you were busy with the secret panel, he mentioned to me and George that his compartment is in the coach next to Julius's. He might hear you open Julius's door."

"I'll be careful, Bess," Nancy promised. "I've got a flashlight, so I won't need to turn on any lights. And I'll wait till it looks like everyone's asleep."

A few hours later Nancy woke up from a doze, still wearing her clothes. Almost twelve, she thought, glancing at her watch. I hope Alden's asleep by now.

Climbing off her narrow bed as the train rumbled and swayed, Nancy pulled out her duffel bag from under the sofa below. After fishing through it for a moment, she drew out a flashlight, then quietly slipped out of the compartment while Bess and George slept.

Nancy walked down the deserted train corridors, keeping an eye out for any signs of activity. The interior lights had been dimmed, and Nancy's shadow loomed large beside her as she tiptoed along.

After moving through the empty dining car, Nancy came to the sleeping car in front of Julius's coach. The corridor seemed endless as she hurried down it, expecting Alden to fling open his compartment door at any moment.

To her relief, she reached the end of the car undisturbed and slid open the outside door. For a moment Nancy stood between the cars, listening to the train chugging and bouncing over the tracks in the late night emptiness. Out the window, vast fields slid by in the moonlight, as flat and dark as lake water.

Once in Julius's car, Nancy flicked on her flashlight and moved toward the bed. After pulling the wooden handle just as Alden had done, Nancy eased the bed out of its nook until it lay on the sofa. She pushed on the panel carved with the eagle and held her breath as it slid open.

As Nancy shone her flashlight into the dark space, a jolt of surprise shot through her. The letters were gone!

A sudden crunching noise sounded from outside—from the rear of the train, Nancy thought.

She flicked off her flashlight, shut the secret panel, then lifted the bed back into its nook. By the light of the moon pouring in through the windows, Nancy decided to take a quick peek at the platform at the very end of the car—and the train. She made her way to the door and cupped her hands next to her face. Pressing her nose against the glass, she peered outside.

A short elderly woman in a lacy nightgown stood on the narrow platform behind the door. The wind whipped through her violet-tinted white hair as she held her face up to the brilliant night sky.

Nancy slid the door open as quietly as she could. Outside, silver-colored train tracks streamed behind them as the train glided through the silent countryside.

The woman stepped closer to the edge of the platform, and Nancy's heart leaped into her throat.

The woman was about to jump!

# 4

## Disaster before Dinner

Nancy bit her lip, worried that any sound could startle the woman into falling. With her leg propping the door open, she leaned forward. Then, in a lightning-quick motion, she grabbed the woman by the wrist and yanked her back to safety.

The woman stared at Nancy, her pale, wrinkled face a mask of absolute shock. Without wasting another second, Nancy pulled her inside the car.

"I'm sorry," Nancy began. "I didn't mean to scare you, but you were right on the edge of the train platform. I was worried you were going to fall."

The woman swiped her forehead with the back of her hand as if brushing cobwebs from her mind. "Oh, my dear," the woman said in a quavery voice. "I had no idea. Thank you so much. I believe you saved my life."

"I'm glad I saw you there," Nancy said.

"Yes, and in the nick of time," the woman pronounced. She shook her head as if trying to wake herself. "It's the most peculiar thing—I haven't the slightest idea why I went out there."

"You don't?" Nancy said.

"Well, I hadn't realized I'd left my bed, much less landed myself in such a dangerous situation," she went on airily. "I guess I must have been sleepwalking. It's a frequent affliction of mine, though I'm terribly embarrassed to admit it."

The tiny woman, who came up to Nancy's chin, stared at Nancy with round, childlike blue eyes. With her thin, knobby fingers, she smoothed down her wispy lavender-tinted hair, which had puffed out like cotton candy from the wind outside.

Nancy studied the woman's wizened face, which seemed almost as fragile and crinkly as parchment.

There was something innocent and endearing about her, Nancy thought, and she seemed totally sincere when she claimed she had been sleepwalking. Still, the woman could have been in Julius's coach around the time that the papers had vanished. She could have stashed them someplace and then hidden outside the moment she heard someone coming. Her sleepwalking could be an act.

Nancy glanced around Julius's coach, searching for signs of pillows or cushions having been hastily rearranged. Everything looked exactly as it had when she had been in the car earlier. She was itching to look around now, but there was no way she could gracefully start searching for the letters as long as the old woman stayed with her.

The old woman sighed. "If you hadn't come along, my dear, I might have woken up as I fell from the train. I would have thought I was having a nightmare, and then realized, all too late, that it was true." She shuddered, clasping her arms against her thin body.

"I think you would have woken up before you fell," Nancy said soothingly, even though she wasn't convinced. "But aren't you cold standing here? Maybe you should go back to your compartment to get some sleep." Nancy picked up her flashlight, which she'd placed on Julius's desk before opening the rear door.

"Yes, that's a splendid idea," the woman said, lightly touching Nancy's arm. "Would you be kind enough to help me back to my compartment, my dear? I'm feeling a bit feeble." Before Nancy could reply, the woman hooked her arm through Nancy's and led her toward the front of Julius's car.

Nancy was surprised at the old woman's strength as they made their way along the length of the coach. She's pulling me instead of letting me help her, Nancy observed—maybe she's just trying to get me out of Julius's coach so I won't find his letters.

Nancy smiled weakly as the woman thanked her for her support. "And now, my dear," the woman said as they stopped outside her compartment in the next car, "there's something I'm curious to know. What were *you* doing in the Van Hoogstraten coach so late at night?"

For a moment Nancy was taken aback by the question. But then a plausible excuse flashed into her mind. "Uh, I lost my keys. I was looking for them in all the places I went tonight," she fudged. "Since I was on a tour of the car earlier, I thought I might have dropped them in there."

"Aha! Well, I saw no keys. But, of course, I was in no condition to observe things either during or after my unfortunate sleepwalking spell." When she cocked her head she reminded Nancy of a curious bird. "Did you find them, by the way?"

"I didn't have a chance to look," Nancy told her, smiling.

"Because you were busy rescuing me," the woman said knowingly. "I'm so sorry to have inconvenienced you, my dear. Take my advice and ask the conductor tomorrow morning whether someone turned them in. All the people I've met on this train seem terribly helpful. And now, where is your compartment? Let me watch you make your way back to it so I can repay your kind favors to me."

"That's not necessary," Nancy began.

"Ah, but it is," the woman said firmly, a half-smile playing about her lips. "Women need to watch out for one another, you know."

Nancy had no choice but to return to her compartment. Once there, she was too tired to sneak back to hunt for Julius's letters, especially when there was only a small chance that she would find them. Lying back on her bed, she relaxed to the chugging rhythm of the train and was rocked to sleep in minutes.

"I never knew train food could include chocolate-chip pancakes," Bess said happily as she poured syrup over the steaming mound on her plate. "Am I in heaven, or what?"

"These waffles aren't bad, either," George pronounced as she dug into them eagerly. "Now, Nan, 'fess up. I woke briefly last night and saw that you weren't in bed. Did you sneak into Julius's coach to read his letters?"

Between mouthfuls of French toast, Nancy told Bess and George about her adventures the night before.

"Do you see the old lady now?" Bess asked, scanning the dining car.

Nancy looked around. "Nope. I haven't seen her yet today. I'll point her out if I do."

"It's no big deal," Bess said with a shrug. "She might have gotten off at an earlier stop, anyway."

"With Julius's letters?" George asked wryly.

"But why would she have wanted to steal his letters?" Bess wondered.

At that moment Alden trooped into the car, dressed in his signature white tie and tails. He stopped at the girls' table and greeted them wearily. "I'm slaving away on these confounded tours until the moment we reach New York this afternoon," he said, "but I'm counting on seeing you at my cousin's party tonight."

"We'll be there," Bess assured him cheerfully

"New York City, next stop," the conductor announced as he marched down the corridor outside the girls' compartment. "New York City, Penn Station, in approximately five minutes."

George heaved her backpack into the corridor while Bess frantically tried to zip up a suitcase that Nancy held closed. "I can't get it," Bess moaned. "I guess the pants that I had on yesterday take up more room than this skirt."

Nancy studied Bess's sleek black knee-length skirt, turquoise tank top, and platform sandals. Her long blond hair was pulled back into an elegant French braid. "You look great, Bess," Nancy told her, "as if you've lived in New York all your life."

"You think so?" Bess said, brightening. She gave her zipper a final, successful tug. "You don't think people will guess I'm really from River Heights?"

"You'll fit in for sure at Dell's party tonight with all those sophisticated people, Bess," George said approvingly. "If you don't pull a muscle from lugging all your suitcases around."

"We'll just have to get a Red Cap," Bess said.

The whistle blew as the train pulled into the station. As soon as the girls stepped off the train, Nancy hailed a Red Cap, who led them through the bustling station and up to the taxi stand.

"I always feel so full of energy here," Nancy commented as their suitcases were being loaded into a taxicab. The girls climbed into the cab, which wasted no time in speeding them toward their destination.

Nancy gazed around at the enormous skyscrapers and swelling crowds of people who pushed their way around the city streets. The air was filled with the sound of honking horns, the subway rumbling underground, and loud exclamations in many different languages.

"It's a great place to visit, but I don't see how people enjoy living here," George said, staring at the noisy crowds thronging the streets. "I mean, it's so crowded, and I bet the cost of joining an athletic club is awesomely expensive."

"But there's no other place as exciting," Bess said, her blue eyes sparkling as she glanced at all the shops.

Ten minutes later the taxi drove down a leafy side street. It stopped outside a large brick apartment building. After paying the cab, Nancy, George, and Bess carried their luggage into the building and on to the elevator. Seconds later they were standing outside Nancy's aunt Eloise's apartment.

The door opened before Nancy even had a chance to ring the bell. A tall, elegant woman in her early forties enveloped Nancy in a huge hug.

"I thought I heard your voices outside," she said warmly, drawing away from Nancy to greet Bess and George. "Come on in, girls. The guest room is all ready for you." Smoothing back her shining brown hair, Aunt Eloise led the girls to their room.

After they were settled, Nancy, George, and Bess joined Nancy's aunt for a cup of tea in her kitchen. Studying their faces, Eloise Drew declared, "You girls look great—it's wonderful to see you all. I hope you remember that my friend Delphinia has invited us all to a dinner dance at her house tonight. It's to celebrate the opening of the Van Hoogstraten Collection next week."

Nancy, Bess, and George told her about meeting Alden Guest on the train. After helping her wash the teacups, they returned to their room to unpack, shower, and dress for the party.

Promptly at seven Nancy, Bess, and George gathered in Nancy's aunt's spacious living room, wearing their long evening gowns.

"Nancy, that peach silk looks absolutely lovely with your strawberry blond hair!" Aunt Eloise exclaimed. "And, George, what marvelous material is your dress made out of?"

George fingered the skirt of her glittery silver dress. "It's something stretchy that doesn't wrinkle—even after two days in a backpack."

"And, Bess," Aunt Eloise went on, "black satin looks smashing on you."

"Thanks," Bess said, pleased. "Black seems like a New York thing, and I wanted to fit in."

After showing off her own green chiffon dress, Aunt Eloise escorted the girls downstairs and into a taxi. Minutes later they arrived at the Van Hoogstraten mansion on Gramercy Park. Surrounded by an elegant wrought iron fence, Gramercy Park was a lush, manicured garden in the midst of a quiet square. Stately old houses and apartment buildings looked onto the park, but the biggest house of all was the Van Hoogstratens'.

"What an awesome place!" Bess cried as she stepped out of the cab into the soft June evening.

Nancy had to agree. Set back from the sidewalk behind a wrought iron fence, the enormous limestone mansion with its intricately carved lintels and columns was magnificent. Its multitude of windows were glowing with yellow light, and the house seemed to welcome visitors to its grand mahogany doors like a queen presiding over a royal banquet.

"This house has twenty bedrooms," Aunt Eloise whispered as they rang the front doorbell, "not counting the servants' wing."

A liveried butler opened the door and ushered them inside. Nancy gazed in awe at her surroundings. Groups of elegantly dressed men and women stood in a huge marble foyer, chatting in low voices while a swing orchestra was playing in the nearby ballroom. A marble staircase swept up to the second floor, flanked by huge bronze candlesticks at its base.

An enormous crystal chandelier hung in the center of the foyer, and paintings that looked as if they had been painted by Renaissance masters hung in gilded frames on the walls. Antique furniture and porcelain brightened the room. The mansion seemed almost alive, as if it had participated in raising several generations of one family. Still, it was so vast that Nancy couldn't believe that Dell could have been happy living in it alone.

To the left of the door was a sturdy walnut desk that Nancy guessed had been set up for the museum—for ticket sales, information leaflets, and the like.

"Eloise!" a woman's voice cried out. "How wonderful to see you." A tall brown-haired woman around Aunt Eloise's age glided over to them wearing a gold silk dress. She had wide cheekbones, an angular face, and a poised manner.

"Dell!" Aunt Eloise said, embracing her friend. "Please meet my niece, Nancy Drew, and her friends, Bess Marvin and George Fayne."

"How nice to meet you," Dell said warmly, shaking the girls' hands. "I've heard so many wonderful things about all of you. Won't you have some champagne, Eloise? And girls, sodas or sparkling cider?"

Before anyone could answer, a creaking noise erupted from above them. Nancy looked up, startled by the loud tinkling of glass. Nancy gasped. The huge chandelier in the center of the ceiling was dangling on a broken chain. Before she could alert Dell, the chain suddenly broke. The lights fizzled as the electric cord snapped from the chandelier's weight.

Like a gigantic spider poised to embrace them with sharp deadly legs, the chandelier was plunging toward them!

# 5

# A Wild Accusation

"Look out!" Nancy yelled. "The chandelier's falling!"

Screaming in panic, guests scattered to the edges of the room as the chandelier crashed down and the orchestra abruptly stopped playing. Shards of crystal skimmed across the marble floor, like schools of tiny sharks heading for a kill.

"Ouch!" a woman said, jerking her ankle upward to inspect a painful-looking gash. She slumped down on a nearby chair, then took a handkerchief from her purse and pressed it to her wound. "Dell, are you trying to punish me for not wearing a long dress tonight?" she asked, smiling feebly.

Nancy could tell the woman was trying to be brave, though her forced smile showed that the cut must have been hurting.

Dell ran over to the woman and offered first aid, as well as a flurry of apologies. Curious to inspect the chandelier, Nancy lifted her skirt above the glass-littered floor and walked gingerly over to it. In the dim light of the wall sconces, Nancy could make out something white in the middle of the ruined crystal.

She leaned over it. Her stomach knotted as she realized what it was—an envelope impaled upon a piece of crystal.

Nancy eyed the fallen chandelier, which resembled a jumble of jagged stalagmites reaching up to stab her with their razor-sharp points. Very carefully she pulled the envelope off the piece of crystal without cutting herself.

Straightening, Nancy ripped open the envelope and scanned the typed note. "The day the Van Hoogstraten house opens to the public will spell its doom!" she read.

Nancy frowned at the strange message. Folding up the note again, she placed it back into the envelope and gazed over at the broken chandelier chain and electrical wire. The wire looked frayed, she observed, as if it could have broken from the weight of the chandelier. But the clean break of the chain suggested that someone had deliberately used a heavy duty wire cutter on it.

Nancy walked over to Dell, who was supervising a middle-aged man bandaging the woman's cut.

Meanwhile, two waiters started sweeping the broken glass into dustpans. A third appeared with a wheelbarrow and heaved the arms and body of the chandelier into it.

The orchestra struck up a lively tune, and the mood of the party immediately changed back to festive. Guests streamed into the ballroom to dance.

"Dell," Nancy said tensely, "there's something I'd like to show you."

Dell smiled fleetingly. "I'm sorry, Nancy, but I need a minute."

"I understand," Nancy said. "But when you have a chance, I thought you'd like to know that this has to do with the chandelier accident."

Dell turned pale. "I hope it's not something bad. I can't take more stress, especially at a party that was supposed to show off this house."

"Don't mind me, Dell, darling," the injured woman said gamely. "I'm as good as new, and I refuse to leave the house tonight until I've worn out my shoes dancing. Why don't you go find out what this young lady has to say?"

Dell smiled. "Thanks, Eleanor, but there's no reason why you and Fred can't find out, too." She turned her lively green eyes on Nancy and said, "Fire away, Nancy. I promise you that whatever your news is, the three of us can handle it."

41

Nancy hesitated. She was uncomfortable having an audience, but feeling she had no choice, she handed the envelope to Dell.

Dell read the note out loud. Then she looked at Nancy, Eleanor, and Fred in horror.

"What an awful message!" Eleanor exclaimed. "What's the meaning of that rubbish?"

"Nothing darling," the man said. "I'd guess the joker didn't plan for the chandelier to fall at the party. Too risky."

"Whoever did this and wrote that note is trying to keep me and my cousins from opening the Van Hoogstraten Collection to the public," Dell said indignantly. "But we won't be intimidated even by a horrendous stunt and a ridiculous message like that!"

"Do you have any idea why someone would want to stop you from opening the museum?" Nancy asked.

"None at all," Dell replied with a puzzled frown.

"It looks as if someone used wire cutters on the chain," Nancy told her. "But the person would have needed a very tall ladder to get up there, plus a lot of time to cut the chain. Wouldn't you—or someone else—have noticed someone out here?"

Dell chewed her lip thoughtfully, then said, "Earlier today, cleaners from an agency were polishing the chandelier. They set up tall ladders in the middle of this hall. But why would one of the glass cleaners want to prevent our museum from opening?"

"I definitely think you have to tell the agency about the incident and ask them to question their workers," Nancy said, adding, "and the police should be contacted."

"I will," Dell promised. "Tomorrow. I'm sure the cleaning service is closed now, and I suppose I should call the police tomorrow, too, now that we know the chandelier was rigged to fall. But I'm not going to ruin the party by asking them to come by tonight." She sighed and added, "Well, if you're really okay, Eleanor, why don't you and Fred circulate? I'm going to try to forget the whole incident and do some mingling myself to try to raise everybody's spirits."

The group broke up, and as Nancy looked around at the dancers and groups of happily chatting guests, she didn't think that Dell would have any trouble raising people's spirits. It was odd that everyone seemed to have forgotten about the incident already, she mused.

"Hey, Nancy," Bess said as she strolled by arm in arm with Alden Guest, who looked handsome and confident in his tuxedo. "Look who I found."

"Hello there, Nancy," Alden said, beaming. "It's wonderful to see you again. Don't forget—you owe me a dance."

Nancy promised to dance with him later, and he and Bess drifted away.

43

Alone once more, Nancy studied the broken chain dangling forlornly from the ceiling. What was that strange note all about? she wondered. She was tempted to offer Dell help investigating the note, but Dell seemed so preoccupied that Nancy decided not to press her.

I'll come back tomorrow to offer her my help then, Nancy decided—even if George and Bess give me grief about getting involved in another mystery.

A waiter announced dinner, and the guests streamed into the vast dining room, which was filled with circular tables, each seating eight. Placecards had been placed at each table setting, and Nancy found hers at Table Six.

Standing behind her chair, Nancy stole a glance at the placecards on either side of her place. The one on her left said Walter Lang while the righthand one said Violet Van Hoogstraten. Neither name was familiar to her, though she assumed that Violet was a relative of Dell's and Alden's.

"Let me help you with your chair," came a man's voice on her left. Looking over, Nancy saw a short but trim middle-aged man whose close-cropped dark hair was thinning slightly. "I'm Walter Lang," he said, introducing himself. Shooting a look at Nancy's placecard, he added, "And I assume you're Nancy Drew."

"Yes," Nancy said, smiling. She stood aside while

44

he pulled out her chair. As she sat down, she asked, "Do you know who Violet Van Hoogstraten is?"

"She's my fiancée's aunt," he said, sitting down. "She's a sweet old lady, but I'm not sure she's coming tonight. At least, I haven't seen her yet."

"Your fiancée?" Nancy repeated. "Do you mean Dell?"

"The very same," he said, his dark eyes twinkling. "Dell and I are going to be married very soon."

A waiter went around the table placing dinner rolls on butter plates with silver tongs. After he had finished, Nancy turned to Walter and said, "I understand you live in Boston."

"In Cambridge, actually," he replied. "I'm a professor of zoology at a university there. Since I'm tenured, my job is absolutely guaranteed, so it wouldn't make sense for me to move to New York, even though this house would be splendid to live in."

"Do you think Dell will miss it?" Nancy wondered.

Walter shrugged. "She seems perfectly happy to be moving out of it—'time for a change,' she says. I just feel guilty that my situation is so inflexible. If she wants to marry me, she has no choice but to move out of this magnificent house, and I feel bad about that."

"But she does have a choice," Nancy said, smiling. "I mean, obviously she'd rather live in Boston with you than live in this house without you."

"True enough," Walter said, chuckling, as a waiter

45

ladled soup into his bowl. "I'm flattered that she prefers me to her house. But that's love for you—there's no predicting it."

Nancy laughed, amused by Walter's modest charm. As she picked up her soup spoon, a soft voice chirped into her right ear, "Excuse me, Miss Drew, but haven't we met?"

Startled, Nancy turned to her right and saw an elderly woman sitting down in the empty chair. "I'm Violet Van Hoogstraten," the woman went on, "Dell's and Alden's aunt."

Nancy gaped. It was the lavender-haired lady who had almost fallen off the train!

Before Nancy could recover from her surprise, Alden rushed up to Violet, his face a mask of fury as he pointed at her.

"You!" he cried, his finger shaking. "It was you, Aunt Violet, who broke that chandelier. And you did it on purpose!"

# 6

## Sneak Thief

A hush fell over the room.

"Alden," Walter began awkwardly.

"What are you talking about, Alden?" Violet cut in, a bewildered smile playing about her lips. "Breaking what?"

"Stop playing the innocent, Aunt Violet," Alden snapped. "You know perfectly well what I'm talking about—the big chandelier in the great hall that crashed to the floor and almost killed us all. Its chain had been cut—by you, Aunt Violet!"

Violet turned a puzzled face on Nancy and Walter. "What's he talking about?" she asked.

"The big chandelier in the foyer broke earlier tonight," Walter explained. "I guess you weren't here

47

yet, Aunt Violet. It crashed to the floor, and most of the crystal on it shattered."

"Oh, what a shame," Violet began, when Dell rushed over to her and Alden from a nearby table.

"Alden," Dell said, between gritted teeth. "Are you out of your mind? How can you be so cruel to Aunt Violet in front of all our guests? You've embarrassed her terribly."

"Oh, it's all right, Dell dear," Violet said, chuckling. "It takes a lot more than a hot-headed nephew to embarrass me. Plus, I have an announcement to make." To everyone's surprise, Violet rose from her chair, looking demure but confident in a long-sleeved taffeta gown that perfectly matched her lavender hair.

"I want to say a few words to all our lovely guests," she said, tapping her spoon against her water glass to get everyone's attention. "I'm not certain how many of you heard what my nephew said, but he seems to think that *I* cut the chain of that chandelier and caused it to crash to the floor. What I want to say is— he has every reason to suspect me."

A murmur of surprise rose up among the guests. Then the room went absolutely still as everyone hung on Violet's next words.

"Even though I'm innocent of the crime," she went on, "Alden found me climbing down from the ladder that had been placed under the chandelier

48

late this afternoon. So you see, he's not as crazy as he seems."

Titters of amusement rose up among the diners at her pronouncement.

Dell gaped at her aunt as if she couldn't believe her ears. Then, recovering herself, she asked, "But why were you climbing on the ladder, Aunt Violet?"

Violet leaned forward and grinned conspiratorially as if she were about to confess a naughty secret to a group of two hundred people.

"I came to the house this afternoon because I was excited by the party," she said in her clear, tremulous voice. "My mother and father used to have such splendid parties, and I was reminded of them by all the hustle and bustle that was going on here. I wanted to be part of the action, you know, and when I entered the great hall and saw the enormous ladder reaching up almost to the ceiling, I simply couldn't resist climbing it. One rung led to the next, if you will."

She grinned mischievously as some of the guests giggled.

Dell appeared flabbergasted. "Aunt Violet, I can understand why you wanted to come over today, but whatever possessed you to climb up the ladder?"

Violet winked at the crowd and said, "As Sir Edmund Hillary said about Mount Everest, I climbed it because it was there."

"But really, Aunt Violet," Dell said gravely, "you

shouldn't have done that. You could have been seriously hurt."

"Don't be so strict, Dell dear," Violet replied. "When I saw that ladder, I simply had to climb it. I couldn't resist getting an aerial view of the hall. After all, I was a well-known aviatrix in my day, you know," she finished proudly.

Dell pursed her lips, then stole a look at their guests all straining to hear more of her aunt's amusing revelations. With a resigned sigh, Dell murmured, "I think we ought to eat our dinner now, Alden and Aunt Violet. We've shown off our family eccentricities long enough."

Before she returned to her table, Dell grabbed Alden's arm and in a low voice said, "You claim Aunt Violet is senile, but where was your brain during that little scene? Is that the kind of publicity you want for the Van Hoogstraten Collection? And what do you mean by accusing Aunt Violet of cutting the chain on the chandelier—I seriously doubt she was holding wire cutters when you saw her on that ladder."

"N-no," Alden said sheepishly. "She wasn't." Returning to his aunt who had just sat down, he added, "I'm very sorry, Aunt Violet. My parents always say I act impulsively, and I guess they're right."

Violet watched her nephew go back to his table, then leaned toward Nancy. "My family says I'm feather-headed and eccentric," she confessed, "but *I*

50

say my nephew is the one whose brain is addled. He's way too hot tempered, that boy. He has a real New York attitude, just like his great-grandfather did. That's ambition for you. It's not always the most attractive trait, if you ask me."

"But Julius had high standards for his work and wanted to do well," Nancy reasoned. "Isn't that a good thing?"

"Oh my, yes!" Violet said. "And I'm happy for Alden that those same qualities have earned him a fine career in banking. It's just that Alden always wants his way—exactly as his great-grandfather did—and he acts before he thinks. What a shame he's so different from his darling parents—my baby sister and her husband. They live in France. They're very smart to have gotten away from all these family politics."

"Wouldn't you like to live in France to be close to your sister?" Nancy asked her.

Violet's blue eyes were wistful. "Well, you see, I never married, and I've always been extremely attached to my dear niece, Dell, who lost her father, my dear brother. But after she got engaged, there's been a bit of friction between us. I must admit that once Dell marries and moves away, New York simply won't be the same. Maybe I'll move to France then."

After dinner the orchestra struck up a rock tune, and the party heated up. Nancy danced with Alden, and then Bess cut in.

"Nancy," Dell said, walking up to her with George. "George asked me to show her Julius's glass birds. Would you like to see them, too?"

"I'd love to," Nancy said, brightening.

"They're in a room we call the Aviary," Dell said. "This way."

She led the two girls down a long hallway to a closed door. After opening it, she flicked on the lights and stood aside for Nancy and George to pass.

Nancy's eyes widened with astonishment at the sight that greeted her. In the soft light of the wall sconces, about fifty glass birds glistened like multi-colored jewels amid silk foliage that waved in the breeze of a ceiling fan. Their smooth glass bodies curved with delicate precision. Every detail of their beaks, wings, and tails—down to the tiny slice of red and yellow brightening a blackbird's wing—had been lovingly created to mimic a particular species.

Partially constructed glass partitions surrounded certain areas. "We're almost done building the exhibits," Dell explained, "so the public can look but not touch." Stepping into the room, she added, "Julius arranged the room into different habitats to accommodate the various bird species he'd made. Look over here."

She led them to a corner where a waterfall had been rigged to trickle down a wall of rocks. Silk palm trees and jungle vines sheltered parrots, toucans, and other tropical species that Nancy didn't recognize.

"And here's the Mediterranean zone," Dell said, gesturing to a ruby-throated hummingbird hovering over a red silk bougainvillea bush. A nearly invisible thread attached the tiny bird to the ceiling.

"Over here must be the northern woods," George commented, pointing to an owl perched on a branch of a fir tree. Nearby, a loon rested on a glistening glass lake.

Nancy fingered the silk needles of a fir tree and its carved wooden branches and cones, amazed at Julius's artistry and his attention to detail.

"Let's not forget the marshland and the desert zone," Dell said pointing to two nearby habitats. Silk reeds and grasses poked up from a glass marsh, into which egrets and great blue herons had been placed in wading positions. In the desert zone, a beautifully blown roadrunner was poised next to a painted papier-mâché rattlesnake and silk cactus.

"Last but not least is the temperate zone," Dell said, gesturing to a grove of oak and maple trees sheltering various species familiar to Nancy—robins, orioles, blue jays, cardinals, and goldfinches.

"Whew!" George exclaimed, shaking her head in amazement as she gazed around the room. "Julius sure must have been an impressive guy to have made all this."

"This room is awesome—a total wonderland," Nancy declared. "Julius was obviously into both birds and glasswork."

"He was an artist whose favorite pastime was vacationing in exotic places around the world birdwatching," Dell explained.

"What's this?" George asked, stepping over to a pedestal at the front of the room.

On top of it a crystal dove lay upon a green velvet cushion. With its barely detectable light blue hue, the dove looked like a rare aquamarine poised to take flight.

"It's gorgeous," Nancy breathed, staring at it in awe.

"That's Julius's only crystal work," Dell explained. "His masterpiece."

"There you are, girls!" came a voice from the doorway. Nancy turned to see her aunt Eloise, looking tired but happy to see them. "I'm beat from all that dancing. I'm going home, but you're welcome to stay if you'd like."

"That's okay, Aunt Eloise," Nancy said. "I didn't get much sleep last night. I think I'll join you."

"Ditto," George said.

"Good luck prying Bess from the dance floor, though," Aunt Eloise commented wryly. "She and Alden have been dancing up a storm."

Nancy and George thanked Dell for the tour and the party, and Aunt Eloise bid her friend goodbye.

Then they gestured to Bess from the foyer that they wanted to leave.

Smiling radiantly at Alden, Bess joined her friends. Then they all trooped out the door and found a cab to take them home.

"I'd really like to check out SoHo," Bess said eagerly as they ate breakfast in Aunt Eloise's kitchen the next morning. Aunt Eloise had gone out shopping, but she had left cereal, muffins, and eggs for the girls. "The shops there are really cool," Bess went on.

George grunted. "I was hoping to walk across the Brooklyn Bridge. It's such a nice day, and the view of New York harbor from the bridge is awesome. What do you say, Nan?"

"I'll do either—or both," Nancy said, shrugging, "as long as we drop by Dell's house first."

"What for?" Bess asked. "Uh-oh. Does it have something to do with the chandelier?"

Nancy grinned. On their way home from the party last night, she had told Bess, George, and her aunt about the warning note on the chandelier. "I thought I'd at least let Dell know I'm a detective. But she might not want my help."

"Yeah right," Bess grumbled. "Nan, you and mysteries are like ice cream and cake—somehow you just go together."

Half an hour later the three girls arrived by taxi at

Dell's house. Nancy rang the doorbell, and Dell herself opened the door.

Nancy was surprised by the stricken expression on Dell's pale face. "Hello, girls," she said tensely. "I'm sorry, but this isn't a good time for you to visit. Something terrible has just happened."

Nancy felt her stomach turn. "What?" she asked.

Dell's bright green eyes bored into Nancy's. "Julius's rare crystal dove has disappeared."

# 7

## Skeleton with a Message

Nancy gaped at her. "You mean—the dove in the Aviary?"

"Yes," Dell replied. "I never lock that room, but obviously I should have. It never occurred to me that I should lock up a room in my own home."

"When did you last see the dove?" Nancy asked.

"At about ten this morning," Dell said, "when I showed Richard Schoonover into the Aviary."

"Richard Schoonover?" Nancy asked.

Dell sighed. "I'm sorry, Nancy, but I really don't have time for these questions. I've got to alert the police."

"Uh, I don't know whether Aunt Eloise mentioned this to you, but I'm a detective," Nancy said quickly. "I'd like to help you investigate the missing dove—and the chandelier."

Dell's face lit up. "Oh, Nancy, what luck!" she exclaimed. "Now that you mention it, I do remember Eloise's telling me that you're a detective. I've been so busy with my party and the museum opening that I totally forgot. Come on in. You, too, George and Bess."

She moved aside for the three girls to enter the house and then led them toward the Aviary.

"I'm thrilled that you can help me, Nancy," Dell said, "because I really didn't want to call the police. If news of this theft leaked to the public, it wouldn't be good publicity for the museum. That chandelier accident last night was bad enough, and Alden's little spat with Aunt Violet will be making all the gossip rounds, I'm sure. The quieter we can keep our problems here, the better."

"I understand," Nancy assured her.

At the doorway of the Aviary, Bess drew in a quick breath, her eyes round with amazement at her first sight of the gleaming birds in their silk habitats. "Whoa! Was Julius like, a genius or something? These birds are beautiful!" she exclaimed.

Nancy scanned the room as the sunlight poured into it through tall windows. The birds looked different in the daylight, she thought. Last night they'd glittered like jewels in the soft glow of the wall sconces. Now they dazzled the eye with a sharp, steady brilliance, like tiny stained glass windows.

Nancy's gaze moved to the pedestal at the front of the room where the crystal dove had rested. Sure enough, the velvet cushion on top was empty.

Nancy looked at Dell. "You were saying that a man named Richard Schoonover had been here this morning?" she prompted.

"Yes, he's a well-known expert on glass," Dell replied. "He agreed to write up a brochure about our exhibit for visitors. He said he'd need about an hour to take notes, but when I came back at eleven, he was gone—and so was the bird. But his car is still parked across the street."

"Does anyone else have a key to the house?" Nancy asked.

"Violet has a spare key, and so does Alden," Dell answered. "Also my housekeeper, Ms. Brown. But that's all."

Nancy thought for a moment, pulling her shoulder-length hair into a red scrunchie she took from the pocket of her khaki slacks. After a moment she said, "The missing dove and the broken chandelier must be connected. Was Richard Schoonover at your house yesterday, too, Dell?"

"No," Dell said. "Not unless he sneaked in without my knowing."

Privately Nancy wondered if the missing letters

from Julius's secret train panel were also related to these incidents. So many odd things happening to the Van Hoogstratens in less than two days probably wasn't a coincidence, she mused.

"Did you ever get in touch with the cleaning service you mentioned last night?" Nancy asked. "You were going to get them to question their workers."

"I didn't forget your advice to me, Nancy," Dell said wearily. "I called the agency first thing this morning and learned that the two workers who cleaned the chandelier were Russian immigrants who don't speak any English. There's no link that I can see between them and the Van Hoogstratens, so what would be their motive in stopping our museum from opening?"

"It doesn't sound as if they were involved," Nancy agreed. "But they might have noticed something suspicious going on while they were here."

George cut in, "For instance, if Violet is guilty, she could have put the note on the chandelier and then paid one of them to cut the chain."

"George is right," Nancy said. "I think it would be a good idea to call the agency again to see if the workers noticed anything suspicious. And I think you should call Richard Schoonover, too, Dell. Does he have an office?"

"A combination office and store," Dell said. "I'll be right back." She left the Aviary for a moment to make the calls while Nancy, Bess, and George combed the room for clues. Five minutes later Dell returned, and the three girls had found nothing.

Dell shook her head, looking grim. "Sorry, girls. No leads. First, there was no answer at Richard's office—just his voice mail. Then the manager of the agency questioned her workers while I waited. They told her they hadn't seen anyone but me here yesterday. Apparently, they left the house briefly at the end of the day to load cleaning supplies into their parked van. After a quick soda break there, they returned inside to collect their ladder. Violet probably came in and climbed it while they were gone."

George walked toward the Aviary door, swinging her arms impatiently. "I'm itching for some action, guys. That missing dove may be halfway around the world by now, but we'd be stupid not to search the house. Who knows? Richard Schoonover could be hiding out in the attic with the dove as we speak."

Dell drew her dark brows together. "You're right, George, but it's a big house, and it'll take a while to search. So let's break up. George and Bess, you take different parts of the downstairs. Nancy and I will start upstairs."

Nancy followed Dell up the wide marble staircase. Antique tapestries hung from the walls, showing medieval lords and ladies gazing at unicorns and griffins.

What an amazing house, Nancy thought, feeling

awestruck once again by the grandeur of the mansion.

At the top of the stairs a number of doors opened off a huge airy hallway lit by tall arched windows on either side. Brightly colored oriental runners accented the polished parquet floors.

"Let's start checking out these bedrooms," Dell suggested. "You take the right side of the hall, Nancy. Start with the pink room right there. I'll take the rooms on the left. When we're finished, we'll check out the old servants' quarters on the third floor, but I doubt Richard's up there. Those rooms have been closed off for years."

Entering the first bedroom on her right, Nancy found a canopied bed with a pink satin spread and rose-colored walls. She looked under the beds and in the closet, finding no one.

The room next door had light blue walls, twin beds with lace coverlets, and blue chintz drapes on the windows. A silver hairbrush and mirror, monogrammed with the initials JVH lay on an antique bureau. "This must be the blue room," Nancy reasoned as she began to search it.

Once again the room was empty. The next room had apple green walls, a Tiffany lamp on a bedside table, and a green and white needlepoint rug. But just as Nancy was about to enter it, she heard a muffled bang coming from somewhere at the end of the hall.

Nancy jogged toward the sound, which came from behind a closed door several rooms away. Standing outside it, she yanked on the knob. The door didn't budge.

Dell didn't tell me there were any locked rooms up here, she thought. "Mr. Schoonover, are you in there?" she cried, stooping toward the keyhole.

A low, inarticulate sound reached her ears. Facing the hallway, Nancy shouted for Dell, who immediately popped out of one of the bedrooms, looking exasperated.

"If you're calling me, Nancy, I can't hear a word you're saying."

"Do you have a key to this lock?" Nancy yelled. "I'm hearing weird sounds from behind this door."

Without wasting another moment, Dell raced over to Nancy. Her normally tidy dark hair straggled in various directions from a barrette at the nape of her neck.

"Richard! Mr. Schoonover! Are you in there?" Dell shouted, pounding on the door.

A low animallike grunt came from inside. "Any skeleton key will fit this door," Dell announced, taking a thin old-fashioned looking key from the pocket of her slacks with shaking hands. Within seconds she had unlocked the door and flung it open.

On the floor of a large linen closet, a man was crouching among fallen sheets, his arms tied behind his back. A dirty cloth was tied across his mouth, and he looked up at Nancy and Dell with a terrified expression in his watery blue eyes.

But it was another sight that really surprised Nancy. On the floor by the older man's feet lay a bird skeleton—a crow, she guessed, from its size—with a piece of paper impaled upon a stiff, skinny claw.

Dell's voice trembled with shock as she said, "Richard Schoonover, how awful! What happened to you?"

# 8

## A Terrifying Call

Bending forward, Nancy worked quickly to untie the man's wrists. The moment she removed the rope the man jumped to his feet and ripped off his gag, the expression in his eyes changing from fearful to furious in less than a second.

"What is the meaning of this, Delphinia!" he snarled as spit flew from his lips. "Are all guests tied up and flung into closets at the famous Van Hoogstraten house? Well, you can take your ancestor's stupid bird collection and stuff it! Expect to hear from my lawyer."

With those words, he picked up the bird skeleton and threw it at Dell, barely missing her. Then he stomped out of the closet and marched down the hall toward the stairway.

Nancy shot a glance at Dell, who was frozen with shock at the man's outburst.

Approaching the stairway, Mr. Schoonover punched the air with a fist as if daring the world to defy him.

Dell snapped to attention with the angry gesture. "Richard!" she cried, rushing after him. "I'm terribly sorry if you were hurt. But you can't go yet. I've got some questions for you."

Mr. Schoonover wheeled around. "You think I care about your questions? Just get me out of here. Please!"

"First, tell me what happened," Dell said, catching up to him. "Who did this dreadful thing to you?"

He turned fierce eyes upon her. "For all I know, you did it, Delphinia!"

"Me?" Dell said, aghast. She squared her shoulders, as if trying to assert her authority. "I'm sorry for what happened to you, Richard, but blaming me is ridiculous. My great-grandfather's crystal dove is missing, and you were the last person seen with it. You've got to answer my questions."

"I'm not staying here another second!" he declared. "After the treatment I received, I don't have to do anything."

"Please cooperate, Richard," Dell said, looking frustrated, "or I'll have to call the police."

Mr. Schoonover gaped at Dell, his face turning crimson with fury. He drew himself up as far as his squat frame would allow and said, "The police? I have never been so insulted in all my life. Are you accusing me of stealing the dove? Because if you are, I'll sue you for libel."

"I'm not accusing you of anything," Dell said calmly. "I'd just like to know what happened in the Aviary. How did you end up in that closet?"

"Beats me," Mr. Schoonover grumbled, calming down slightly. He shot a sudden glance at Nancy. "Who's she?" he asked sharply.

"This is my friend Nancy Drew," Dell replied, placing an arm around Nancy's shoulders. "She happened to be visiting me when I realized that both you and the crystal dove were missing. She helped me look for you."

Mr. Schoonover glared at Nancy as Dell continued, "Nancy, I'm sure you realize that this is Richard Schoonover, the expert on glass artifacts who's writing our brochure. Coincidentally, he's also a descendant of Gustav Kinderhook, the glass blower with whom my great-grandfather apprenticed long ago in Holland."

"That is a coincidence," Nancy said pleasantly, extending her hand for Mr. Schoonover to shake. "It's very nice to meet you."

Mr. Schoonover seemed to soften. "Won't you tell us what happened?" Nancy asked him, smiling. Mr.

Schoonover sighed. "I was taking notes on Julius's collection—standing in front of his crystal dove. And then—I don't remember anything more until I woke up in that closet with a lump on the back of my head." Gingerly he rubbed his head and winced.

Nancy frowned. "So obviously someone hit you, took the crystal dove, and then locked you in the closet. But what about the bird skeleton? Where did that come from?"

"I don't know," Mr. Schoonover said in a puzzled tone. "The closet was dark, and when I finally came to, I didn't notice the skeleton—not until you two opened the door and I threw it at you."

Nancy studied the older man. Could he be lying about being attacked? she wondered. After all, Mr. Schoonover was the last person seen with the dove. But then how could he have staged his imprisonment in the closet after he'd stolen it?

Nancy held up her finger. "Wait a second," she said, then walked back down the hall to the skeleton. Bending down, she removed the paper from the bird's claw and scanned it.

" 'Stay away from Julius's birds, Schoonover, or you'll end up like this one,' " she read.

Nancy showed the note to Dell and Mr. Schoonover. After reading it, Schoonover crumpled the paper in a violent gesture, as if he were squeezing someone's neck. His eyes flashed fiercely as he snapped, "What is the meaning of this drivel? I'm going to get the skunk who wrote that rot if it's the last thing I do! Richard Schoonover does not allow threats to go unpunished."

"May I have the note, please?" Nancy asked, extending her hand. "It may turn out to be an important clue."

"No!" Mr. Schoonover growled, pocketing the note. "I'll take no chances—such an insult must never become public." He turned and stormed down the stairs, adding, "I will never set foot inside this house again. Anyone who even thinks I may have stolen that dove will face a lawsuit for libel!"

Dell and Nancy traded glances. Then they followed Schoonover downstairs to make sure he was really leaving. Just as he approached the front door, it swung open, nearly knocking him over.

Alden stepped inside as Mr. Schoonover recovered his balance and brushed by him. "Careful, young man," Mr. Schoonover snapped. "You almost hit me." After hurrying outside, he slammed the door shut.

Alden fixed his clear hazel eyes on his cousin. "Did you allow Schoonover in here, Dell?" he asked. "I'm surprised at your poor judgment."

Dell looked at Alden coolly. "May I remind you, Alden, that you're the one who complained that we had no brochure to give our museum visitors? Since you never got around to writing one, I hired Richard

Schoonover for the job. You can't argue with getting the best."

"But Schoonover's the worst possible person to write our brochure," Alden said, regarding Dell as if she were a total idiot. "You know that he's insanely jealous of Julius."

"Oh, that old rumor," Dell said, waving her hand dismissively. "Mr. Schoonover's a professional. He's not going to let an old family grudge get in the way of his judgment."

At that moment Bess and George joined the group. "Did you find him?" Bess asked.

"We found him and he's gone already," Nancy answered, then added to Alden, "What grudge?"

"Richard Schoonover is jealous of what Julius became," he explained. "He's annoyed because Julius got to be rich and famous while his own ancestor—Julius's teacher—stayed poor and unknown in Holland."

"So did Schoonover have the crystal bird?" George cut in, looking at Nancy and Dell.

"No," Dell said with an anxious glance at Alden.

"What bird?" Alden asked, frowning.

Dell filled him in on the missing dove, and then updated Bess and George on what had happened upstairs with Mr. Schoonover.

"Well, this is just great!" Alden snapped, his eyes dark with fury. "The prize piece of our collection disappears days before the museum is set to open. Nice going, cousin."

"Alden, calm down," Dell ordered. "Your sarcasm isn't going to help us find the dove."

"Isn't it obvious that Schoonover swiped it, stashed it in his car or something, and then faked his attack with the aid of an accomplice?" Alden took out a hankerchief and mopped his brow. Drawing in a deep breath, he struggled to control his anger.

"I'm sorry, Dell," he continued in a softer tone. "I have no right to speak to you that way. But I care so much about Julius's collection, and we've both worked so hard to get it ready for the public. I'll feel crushed if we don't get a good response from the critics and public."

"Relax, Alden. I'm sure we will," Dell said soothingly.

"I hope so," Alden said. "I feel as if Julius would be disappointed with us if we fail. And with the crystal dove missing, we're sunk."

"Just pull yourself together, Alden, and we'll hope for the best," Dell said. "Anyway, one missing object won't decide the museum's fate—even if it was the crown jewel in our collection. And if we're going to find the dove, we all need to stay calm."

"I'm going after Schoonover," Alden broke in. "He's probably heading for his office with the dove right now. See you later." And he rushed out the front door.

71

Once he had left Dell turned to Nancy, Bess, and George. "Don't mind Alden," she said with a sigh. "He works hard and means well, but he's also kind of hotheaded at times. Won't you girls stay for lunch? It's the least I can do, and I'd like to discuss the case with you."

After making a lunch of leftovers from the party, Dell placed the cold meats and bread on a tray with a pitcher of lemonade and some cookies. Then she led the girls out to a back patio beautifully planted with herbs and flowers and set the tray on a glass-topped table.

Everyone had been eating in silence for a few minutes when Nancy turned to Dell and asked, "So what specifically did you want to discuss with us?"

Dell shrugged. "Schoonover's role in it, I guess. I mean, I think I do agree with Alden that Schoonover could be guilty. It's well-known that he's always been jealous of Julius's reputation. But then I tell myself he's a respected glass expert, and I could never imagine his personal feelings getting the better of him."

"And I'm sure it never occurred to you that he might steal," Bess chimed in. "If you'd thought that was a risk, you never would have hired him."

"But I probably should have been more cautious," Dell admitted. "I mean, we're only human, and maybe his jealousy just got the better of him. I should have realized that could happen."

72

"When the Van Hoogstraten Collection opens to the public, Julius will be even more famous," George said. "That could be making Schoonover crazy."

"Yeah, and he could be desperate to keep the museum from opening," Bess offered.

A cordless phone rang from a side table next to Nancy. "Would you mind getting that, Nancy?" Dell asked, munching on her salad. "My mouth is full."

"Sure," Nancy said, picking up the phone. "Hello?" she said into the mouthpiece.

"Dell darling," said a creepy, muffled voice. "Remember your precious Walter? Well, you won't be seeing him any time soon."

"Who is this?" Nancy said, but the line went dead.

# 9

## Danger on the Bridge

Nancy hung up the phone, her mind clicking away. She hadn't recognized the caller's voice. She hadn't even been able to tell whether the person was a man or a woman. But from the sound of the message, Nancy guessed that the caller had kidnapped Walter.

"Who was that, Nancy?" Dell asked.

Nancy braced herself to give Dell the bad news. "I don't know," she said gravely. "But whoever it was may have kidnapped Walter. We've got to call the police."

"Kidnapped Walter?" Dell said, shooting up from her chair. She spilled her food over the patio stones as Bess and George stared at Nancy in stunned silence. "Why? Nancy—tell me exactly what the message was."

Nancy repeated the brief conversation.

Dell slumped back down in her chair. Then she turned a hopeful face on Nancy and added, "The words 'any time soon' suggest that Walter is alive. It sounds as if he's been kidnapped, but at least he's alive! Oh, Nancy, we've got to find him," Dell said plaintively.

"When did you last see him?" Nancy asked, sitting down in her chair.

Dell leaned back, her hand on her forehead, eyes shut. "My mind is whirling," she moaned. "I don't know if I can stand this. Poor Walter."

"Dell," Nancy said gently. "You've got to pull yourself together so we can find him. Please answer me."

Dell sighed, her eyes still shut. "I'm sorry, Nancy. I'll try my best. I last saw Walter this morning at about ten. He told me he was going out for a walk downtown to visit a colleague. Someone must have kidnapped him along the way."

Nancy picked up the cordless phone and punched in 911. "Before we do anything else, I'm calling the police," she declared.

Fifteen minutes later two police officers arrived at the Van Hoogstraten house. They introduced themselves to Dell and the girls as Detective Martha Phillips and Officer Juan Serrano.

The police officers listened attentively as Dell

and Nancy told them about the chandelier incident and the strange phone message. Dell also explained that since Walter was visiting her from Boston, he had no office or hotel in New York where he might check in.

"He was planning to do some research at the Bronx Zoo," Dell told them, "but he hadn't started it yet. There's no other place he could be except here or sightseeing."

The police explained that usually a person had to be missing for forty-eight hours before they took the disappearance seriously. However, since Dell had received a mysterious and threatening phone call suggesting that Walter had been kidnapped, they agreed to start looking for him immediately.

"As long as you're sure that Mr. Lang isn't pulling a practical joke," Detective Phillips said, "we'll do our best to find him."

"Walter would never joke about something like this!" Dell cried. "He's a responsible person, and I'm sure he's in danger."

"Then we'll do what we can to find him, Ms. Van Hoogstraten," Officer Serrano assured her.

As Dell was showing the police officers out the front door, Nancy turned to Bess and George and whispered, "Why don't we leave, too? I really want to talk about this case with just you guys—away from Dell."

Before Bess and George could respond, the front door burst open, and Dell stumbled back against the girls.

"Oh, I'm so sorry, Dell," said the thin, reedy voice. Violet Van Hoogstraten peeped around the door frame and added, "This door is like a weapon. I didn't realize anyone was behind it. Is everyone quite all right?"

"We'll live, Aunt Violet," Dell said, managing a weak smile.

"Good," Violet declared as she marched into the foyer, carrying a bundle of mail. "Here's your mail, Dell. I ran into the letter carrier on the sidewalk. He knows I'm family." As she dumped the mail into her niece's hands, Violet's tiny brow crinkled under her lavender fringe. "By the way, what were the police doing on your front steps?"

Dell wasn't listening. With her face sheet white, she held up a letter with no stamp. "Van Hoogstraten Family" was printed on it in block letters.

She plunked the pile of mail down on a nearby table and tore open the envelope. " 'To all of Julius Van Hoogstraten's descendants,' " she read aloud. " 'If his house is opened to the public, I will curse you forever!' "

"What a dreadful letter," Violet said, placing a hand over her heart. "Who would send such a thing to you, Dell darling?"

"To *us*, Aunt Violet," Dell said. "It's addressed to all of Julius's descendants."

Violet picked up a piece of junk mail and began to fan herself with it. "Such a shocking message! I feel faint, dear," she warbled. "I must lie down. What does it mean we'll all be cursed?" She toddled off to a sofa in the adjoining parlor and eased herself on to it.

"Oh, my goodness!" Dell exclaimed, her gaze shooting back to Nancy, George, and Bess. "I just remembered—Richard Schoonover's store is in SoHo. It's called the Glass Slipper. His office is in the back of the store. Since Walter said he was going downtown, maybe he went into the Glass Slipper and Richard kidnapped him—if Alden is right about Richard's stealing the dove. He could have stashed Walter in his office, or in the basement."

Nancy chewed her lip, thinking about Dell's words and trying to picture the older Schoonover overpowering Walter. "Hmm, the anonymous phone call came about an hour after Mr. Schoonover left," she said. "How far is SoHo from here?"

"Minutes by car or cab," Dell said. "Richard would have had plenty of time to drive back to his store, kidnap Walter, and then make the phone call."

The front door shot open, and Alden hurried inside. His chestnut hair was tousled, and his normally relaxed face was drawn with worry. "I never caught up with Schoonover," he announced breathlessly. "When I went down to the Glass Slipper, the door was locked. Where could he be with that dove?"

"The dove isn't the only thing he may have taken," George cut in.

Alden shot George a quizzical look, and Dell told him the news about Walter.

Alden's eyes widened as she spoke. But before he could say anything, Dell handed him the note addressed to Julius's descendants.

Alden scanned it, then slapped the paper with the back of his hand. "We'll all be cursed?" he cried. "What is this? I mean, Schoonover *must* be guilty— he's so jealous of Julius's glass birds that he'll do anything to keep the rest of the world from seeing how great they are. That's why he doesn't want us to open the museum, and I'll bet he kidnapped Walter just to prove his point."

"We don't know why Walter was kidnapped," Nancy said. "The caller never told Dell to do anything special to get him back, like leave money somewhere or give up plans for the museum."

"That's weird," Bess commented. "Maybe the person just forgot to say what he or she wanted."

Nancy shrugged. "Maybe." She shot a knowing

look at George and Bess and murmured, "We haven't been outside all day, and I could use some exercise. How about a walk across the Brooklyn Bridge?"

"Great idea, Nan," George said brightly.

Bess opened her mouth to protest when George nudged her ankle with the toe of her sneaker. "Great idea, Nancy," Bess echoed, forcing a grin.

The girls said goodbye to Dell and Alden and explained that they'd be in touch, that they just had to get a little exercise. "Don't worry, Bess, I don't want to walk on the bridge right now," Nancy assured her once they were outside. "I want to check out the Glass Slipper without Dell or Alden tagging along."

George shook her head sadly. "I guess a walk across the bridge was too good to be true," she said in a wistful tone.

Nancy took a map of Manhattan out of her purse and located the nearest subway that would take them to SoHo. Then she slipped into a coffee shop and asked to use a phone book.

"The Glass Slipper is on Spring Street," she told Bess and George as she found the listing. "Luckily the subway stops right near there."

Five minutes later Nancy, Bess, and George were rattling through a dark tunnel on a crowded subway heading south. "This is surreal," Bess whispered as they hung on to a metal pole to keep their balance as the train swayed.

About four stops later Nancy said, "Hey, guys, this is us—Spring Street."

Soon Nancy, George, and Bess were walking down Spring Street looking for the Glass Slipper.

"Look at the handbags in this window, guys!" Bess exclaimed. "And the jewelry. Maybe I'll stop in here later. Wow—this restaurant looks pretty cool." She stopped outside a trendy bistro with polished brass doors. Young people blithely sipped lattes at tables outside while talking into cell phones.

Nancy grabbed Bess's arm. "Come on, Bess. We can come back later."

"Come on, I found it," George called, motioning with her hand from halfway down the block.

Nancy and Bess hurried to join her outside a small unassuming storefront. *The Glass Slipper* was written in delicate gold script across the front door. Antique glass and crystal ware sparkled behind a large show window.

As Nancy pushed open the door, a bell on it tinkled, announcing their presence. Richard Schoonover appeared through a back door, which he immediately closed behind him.

His eyes widened as he recognized Nancy. "Well, well—it's Ms. Van Hoogstraten's friend. How can I help you?"

"Delphinia told us about your store," Nancy said, "and we were shopping in SoHo anyway, so we decided to check out some of your stuff."

Mr. Schoonover blinked at them in surprise. "You girls are interested in buying antique glassware?" he asked suspiciously. "It doesn't seem like something kids your age would want."

"Uh, my dad collects crystal," Nancy fudged, "and I thought I'd take him home a memento from New York."

"Really?" Mr. Schoonover said, his ice blue eyes narrowing as he glared at her doubtfully.

"Yes," Nancy went on, ignoring his sarcasm. She peered into a glass display case at some crystal finger bowls and asked, "You have beautiful stuff here, Mr. Schoonover, but I don't see anything for my dad. Do you have more merchandise in the back?"

"That depends," he said coolly. "What would be right for your dad?"

"Uh, animals. Glass animals. Do you have any in the back?"

Mr. Schoonover drummed his fingers impatiently on the countertop. "Why is it that I don't believe you? Maybe because I have the feeling that you're really looking for Delphinia's crystal dove. I'm not a fool, Ms. Drew. I have no doubt that she sent you here. So the answer is no, I don't have any merchandise for sale in the back. Only what you see here."

Nancy sighed. Mr. Schoonover wasn't being exactly cooperative—maybe because he really did have something to hide in the back office, she concluded.

Nancy decided to try another tack. Remembering Alden's claim that the store had been locked up earlier, Nancy said, "We tried coming here right after you left the Van Hoogstratens. But the store was locked. Were you out to lunch?"

"It's none of your business where I was!" he retorted. "We obviously just missed each other. Your method of transportation must have been faster than my car. The traffic was frightful today. Now, if you're not prepared to buy anything, I really must ask you girls to leave. I'm too busy to answer any more of your questions."

"Sorry if we bothered you," Nancy said as Mr. Schoonover grunted a curt goodbye.

Opening the door Nancy said, "Maybe we should get coffee at that café you liked, Bess."

"Hey, what about our walk across the Brooklyn Bridge?" George protested. "If I don't get some exercise soon, I'll go insane."

"Count me out," Bess said as they walked out the door. "I mean, right now we're within easy walking distance of the cutest stores in the world—not to mention the best pastries—and you guys want to walk across a bridge? Some choice!"

George peeled a few dollars from her wallet and handed them to Bess. "If you come across any éclairs, Bess, nab one for me. How about you, Nan?"

Nancy grinned. "I wouldn't turn one down, Bess," she said, handing her some cash. "Thanks. Shall we meet you back at Aunt Eloise's later?"

"Okay, but I'll be at least a couple of hours prowling around here," Bess said happily, before wandering down the street in the opposite direction.

A half hour later Nancy and George were leaning over the railing of the Brooklyn Bridge, drinking in the beautiful view of the harbor, the Statue of Liberty, and the Manhattan skyline. Graceful sailboats carved paths through the shimmering water alongside chunky ferries, while the lowering sun threw extravagant streaks of pink light across a turquoise sky. The towering skyscrapers of the financial district seemed to stare at the girls, their glowing windows like thousands of tiny bright eyes peering from colossal mounds of granite.

People streamed along the pedestrian walkway on their way home from work, jostling the girls as they hurried along. Below the walkway was the road, on which cars rushed from Manhattan to Brooklyn and back. Nancy tried to ignore the noise and concentrate on the view.

All at once she felt a shove from behind. It was

someone's hand, she realized, jamming into her back. Her arms shot out as she tried to get her balance—but it was too late. She toppled over the railing.

Nancy grabbed wildly at the base of the railing as she slid forward, trying to use it to stop her descent. She clutched it with one hand as her legs swung madly and she dangled over a lane of traffic rushing below her!

# 10

## Surprise at the Door

Nancy forced her gaze upward as she clung to the railing, its metal edges digging into her hands. George leaned over the railing and reached down to help, but no matter how far she stretched, her fingertips remained inches from Nancy's hands.

Nancy's palms were slick with perspiration. With every ounce of energy she had, she concentrated on maintaining her grip. Otherwise, she knew her hands would slip and she'd be lost.

"Help!" she heard George cry out from above. "Help! My friend has fallen from the bridge. She's clinging to the base of the railing. Someone's got to help us—now!"

Seconds later two young men with dreadlocks peered over the railing at Nancy. "Avery!" shouted the one on the left. "You and this young lady here—you hold my legs as I lean over the bridge. I think I can lift her up if you hold me tight."

"Okay, John, we've got you," his friend declared.

As George and Avery held on to him, John inched himself over the railing until it pushed against his waist. George's face turned red with the strain of John's weight. Cautiously John reached toward Nancy and grabbed her wrists. "Let go," he gasped. "I've got you."

Taking a deep breath and closing her eyes, Nancy let go of the railing. She felt a momentary relief as she realized that she wasn't falling.

Tilting his face toward George and Avery, John shouted, "Hold on to me tight—I'm pulling her up!"

Nancy felt John's powerful arms slowly lifting her. The moment she could get a toehold on the bottom of the railing, she helped him out by pushing herself upward.

Seconds later Nancy was scrambling over the railing to safety. Her legs felt like jelly as she drew in deep ragged breaths of air, but she forced herself to keep her wits about her.

"How are you, Nan?" George asked, her hands on Nancy's shoulders as she peered at her with concern and relief. "Thank goodness John and Avery came along."

"I'm okay," Nancy said gamely. Turning to John

and Avery, she added, "Thank you so much for rescuing me. I would have fallen and been killed if you guys hadn't come along."

"Did you see who pushed Nancy?" George asked the two guys.

Avery shook his head. "No, I didn't even notice that someone had fallen until you yelled for help."

"Same here," John said.

"I saw this shadow out of the corner of my eye just before I was pushed," Nancy told them. "But I never got to see who it was."

Crowds of people continued across the bridge on their way home from work as Nancy, George, John, and Avery stood talking. "Look at all these people," George commented, "and not one of them came forward to give us any info about your attacker, Nan."

John frowned. "Maybe no one noticed the attack," he offered. "It's crowded on the bridge at rush hour. There's so much going on in this city that sometimes your senses get bombarded—people have to tune some things out, or else they'd go nuts. A woman being pushed from the bridge would draw people's attention if they saw it, but someone running away probably wouldn't."

"The person who pushed Nancy probably blended into the crowd," Avery said. "But just to prove to you girls that New Yorkers have their good side, why don't you come hear our band play tonight at this club called S.O.I.—stands for Songs of the Islands—compliments of us? We're a Jamaican jazz/reggae band called the John Avery Quartet."

Nancy grinned. "George and I would love to hear you guys. Would it be okay if we brought our other friend, Bess?"

"Sure thing," John said, smiling. He gave the girls directions to S.O.I. before ambling off with Avery across the bridge.

Nancy shot a wry look at George. "I think I've had my fill of the New York skyline for now. What's next, Fayne?"

"Back to your aunt's house to get ready for S.O.I.," George said firmly.

Forty-five minutes later Nancy and George had joined Bess in the kitchen of Eloise Drew's apartment. The three girls were heating up a pizza that Bess had ordered while Nancy filled her in on her Brooklyn Bridge ordeal.

Bess pointed to a small white box and said, "There's an éclair inside that that has your name on it, Nan. I'm prescribing it as the best medicine for what you just went through."

Nancy laughed. "Thanks, Bess. I'm sure I'll be cured soon. And by the way, how was your afternoon?"

"Well, when I got back from shopping, guess who called? Alden," Bess said, her eyes shining.

"Alden? What did he want?" George asked.

"He invited me to take a carriage ride with him in Central Park tomorrow and have tea in the Palm Court at the Plaza Hotel," Bess replied. "It sounds like a fun, fancy New York thing to do—especially because Alden's so cute and sophisticated."

"Yeah, but he's also a suspect, Bess," Nancy warned. "I mean, Alden, Dell, and Violet all knew that we were planning to walk across the Brooklyn Bridge this afternoon. It has to be one of them—I doubt I was attacked by a random stranger."

"But Richard Schoonover knew about the Brooklyn Bridge, too," Bess reminded her. "We talked about our plans in his store as we were leaving."

"That's true—he could have followed us after we left," George said.

"Hey, girls," Aunt Eloise said from the doorway of the kitchen. "How was your day? There was a big sale at Macy's, and I bought out the store." She dropped her two large shopping bags and rubbed her hands together. "Whew, those were heavy. I bought towels, kitchenware, clothes, and even some shoes."

In a low voice Nancy said to Bess and George, "Let's talk about the bridge thing later, guys. I don't want to worry Aunt Eloise."

Nancy smiled. "Bess went shopping, too—in SoHo—while George and I took a stroll across the Brooklyn Bridge. And earlier we saw Dell."

"Oh, really? How is she?"

Nancy filled her aunt in about the strange things that had happened at Dell's house, including Walter's disappearance.

Her aunt's face clouded over. "I understand that you want to investigate the case, Nancy. You are a detective, after all. But please be careful. This person sounds dangerous."

Nancy promised she would be careful. Then she explained that she, George, and Bess were going out for the evening to S.O.I. "Sounds like fun," her aunt said. "I'm going to call Dell and tell her I'll do whatever I can to help Walter."

Half an hour later Nancy, George, and Bess were sitting at a table at S.O.I., sipping sodas. A crowd of young people filed into the club, taking seats at surrounding tables. Some had dreadlocks like John and Avery, while others looked punk with brightly dyed hair and black leather clothes. Still others appeared to be young working professionals. All of them, Nancy thought, seemed eager to see the show.

Nancy checked her watch and said, "It's a quarter of eight—fifteen minutes till the band comes on." Leaning back in her chair, she closed her eyes and added, "It feels great to sit back and relax after such a crazy day. Thank goodness John and Avery came along when they did."

"You're telling me," George said. "Speaking of our crazy day, what do you make of the case so far, Nancy? I mean, who doesn't want the Van Hoogstraten Collection opened to the public—and why?"

"And why was poor Walter kidnapped?" Bess chimed in.

Nancy pushed her hair behind her ears as she thought. "Well, whoever is doing all this must realize I'm investigating the case or I wouldn't have been pushed off the bridge. And since Dell, Alden, Violet, and Mr. Schoonover knew our plans this afternoon, they're our top suspects."

"That seems right," George agreed. "Also, Violet was at the scene of some of the weird things that happened, like when the papers were taken from Julius's secret panel, and she climbed up that ladder to the chandelier."

"Plus, she brought in the pile of mail with the anonymous note in it," Bess pointed out. "But what makes me curious is—why would she be doing all this?"

"Maybe because she doesn't want Dell to get married and move away from New York," Nancy guessed. "She mentioned to me that she and Dell had always been close, and New York City won't be the same for her after Dell moves away."

"So if Dell's house doesn't become a museum, what would happen to it if she moves to Boston?" George wondered.

"It would either be empty, or the Van Hoogstratens would have to sell it," Nancy said, "and Dell might not want to do either of those things."

"Yeah, maybe Violet thinks that if she nixes the museum plan, Dell will change her mind about moving to Boston," George said.

"Hmm," Bess began, "Violet wasn't at the house when Walter disappeared—I wonder if she has an alibi for that time?"

"Even if she doesn't have one, it wouldn't matter," Nancy said. "Violet is so old and frail, I can't see her kidnapping Walter and attacking Mr. Schoonover. I suppose she could have hired someone to do all that stuff for her."

"But why would she have taken the crystal bird?" Bess asked.

Nancy shrugged. "Who knows? But then, why would Alden or Dell have taken it? They're suspects, too."

"And don't forget," George said, "Alden had the opportunity to steal the papers on the train, just as Violet did. He could have cut the chandelier chain after Violet left the room yesterday—he admitted to being at the house when the ladder was up. Plus, he's strong enough to have attacked Mr. Schoonover and kidnapped Walter on his own."

"I don't know, George," Bess said, twirling a strand of long blond hair around her forefinger. "I mean, everything you just said is true, but I think you're being a little hard on the guy. Why would Alden want to close the museum? He's the publicity director. He's devoting two weeks of his vacation to promoting the place."

Nancy took another sip of her soda. "Alden doesn't really have a motive," she agreed. "But Mr. Schoonover does, since he's so jealous of Julius's reputation."

"Julius will probably become world famous the minute everyone discovers how great his birds are," George remarked. "That's going to drive Mr. Schoonover ballistic. He'd do anything to keep people from knowing about Julius and talking up his work."

Nancy cast her mind back to their conversation with Alden on the train. "Remember when Alden told us that only a couple of glass experts have ever seen Julius's birds? So not that many people know about him. But if a bunch of modern critics see the birds and rave about how great they are, everyone will know about Julius."

"A nightmare for Mr. Schoonover," Bess pronounced. Leaning her cheek on her hand, she added, "I can see why Mr. Schoonover may have taken the crystal dove—it's probably really valuable and he could sell it to a glass collector through his store."

"Good thinking, Bess," Nancy said approvingly.

"Now, what about Dell?" George said, changing the subject. "I know she heard us make plans to walk on the Brooklyn Bridge, but does it really make sense that she's a suspect? I mean, why would she want to ruin her own museum?"

Nancy chewed her lip, thinking. "Maybe she's hoping to manipulate Walter into living with her in the mansion instead of in Boston. We just mentioned that if the Van Hoogstraten Collection can't open, Dell might not want to leave the house empty or sell it."

"Yeah, but Dell was with us when Walter was kidnapped," Bess declared. "And she wasn't on the train when the papers disappeared."

"Neither was Mr. Schoonover," George said. "You know, Dell could have an accomplice. She sure has enough money to hire someone."

Before Nancy could comment, the John Avery Quartet filed on to the stage from behind a curtain and took up their places. Nancy noticed that Avery played drums, while John played bass guitar. Another man carried a trumpet, while still another sat down in front of a piano. The audience buzzed with anticipation as the band checked their instruments.

Cupping her hand beside her mouth, Nancy whispered, "I have this major feeling that Julius's missing papers and the crystal dove are important clues to the case. I'm going to do some research on the history of the dove tomorrow."

George gave her the thumbs-up sign, while Bess nodded eagerly. Then the band launched into a song, and the club was immediately quiet. Tapping her foot in time to the rhythmic beat, Nancy stopped thinking about the case for a few hours while she lost herself in the music.

"So how are you going to research the history of that dove, Nancy?" Bess asked as Nancy, Bess, and George piled out of a cab in front of the Van Hoogstraten mansion the next morning.

"I'm going to see if Dell has any of Julius's old letters and papers," Nancy replied. "You never know— maybe there's some information in them about the dove that will give us a clue."

Standing outside the huge oak doors of the house, Nancy rang the bell. Seconds later the door flew open.

Walter Lang stared at her grimly from the foyer.

# 11

## Crazy Horse

"Excuse me, Nancy," Walter said in a clipped tone. "Please let me by."

With his gaze set and his lips pressed firmly together, Walter brushed past Nancy, George, and Bess and raced down the flight of marble steps to the sidewalk below. Nancy quickly lost sight of him as he threaded his way east among a crowd of other pedestrians.

"Walter?" George said, sounding stunned.

"Am I seeing things?" Bess murmured.

Dell appeared at the door. "What's the story with Wal—" Nancy began, then stopped at the sight of Dell's stricken face. Tears glistened at the corners of her eyes, and her mouth trembled as she invited the girls inside.

Dell led the way to a cozy sitting room off the foyer. "Alden and I have been using this room as the museum office," Dell explained as she motioned for the girls to sit down on a sofa. "It's where we've been working on museum press releases and finances and stuff like that." She took a tissue from a box on a desk and blew her nose as she eased herself into an armchair.

"Tell us about Walter, Dell," Nancy asked. "Obviously, he's back."

"In a manner of speaking," Dell said mournfully. Taking a deep sigh, she explained, "I was eating breakfast in the kitchen this morning when the front doorbell rang. I nearly fainted with surprise when I opened the door and saw Walter. I was so happy that I threw myself into his arms, but—" She paused, dabbing at her eyes with another tissue. "Oh, it's too embarrassing—I can't go on."

Nancy felt a pang as she watched Dell bite her lip to keep from crying. "You don't have to be embarrassed in front of us, Dell," she said gently.

"Oh, I know, Nancy." Dell sniffed, forcing her lips into a smile. "Thanks for the reassurance. Anyway, I have to tell you what happened because if you're going to solve this case, you'll need to know all the details." Dell took a deep breath and continued, "I knew right away that something was wrong when Walter came in today. He's always been very affectionate, but when I tried to hug him, he pulled away from me. And every time I tried to look him in the eyes, he averted his gaze. It was weird."

"Oh, Dell—how awful!" Bess said sympathetically.

"It *was* awful," Dell said. "Walter kept me at arm's length and looked at me as if I were a total stranger. Then he told me that we needed to talk. My heart was hammering as I followed him into the kitchen, but somehow I managed to ask him where he'd been and if he was all right."

"What did he say?" Nancy asked.

"Just as we suspected, he'd been kidnapped, but he refused to tell me who had done it," Dell replied. "He said it didn't matter because he was okay. He even asked me to call off the police. And then—"

Dell paused, her face tightening as she added, "He broke off our engagement!"

"No!" Bess said, looking stricken.

"Oh, Dell, I'm so sorry," Nancy said, while George shook her head gravely.

"He told me that he still loved me," Dell explained, "but he thought our backgrounds were too different for the marriage to work."

"Your backgrounds are too different?" George echoed, sounding puzzled. "What does he mean by that?"

Dell shook her head, clearly bewildered. "Walter comes from more modest beginnings and he went to college on a scholarship, but we definitely have the same interests. I mean, we like the same people and books and movies and restaurants—all that stuff. And we both love animals and the outdoors. He thinks he'll be taking me away from my house and my fancy life, but I want to live more like a regular person, anyway."

Gesturing around the room with her hand, she added, "I never asked for any of this. Sure, the house is beautiful, but so what? I don't want to live like some relic in a museum. All I want is Walter."

Nancy sighed. It was true that Dell lived in a spectacular house, but what was the point if she was lonely? "So Walter didn't say anything about how he got kidnapped?" she asked.

"Nope," Dell said, "and he was adamant that we call off the police. He claimed he was harmlessly detained, and he totally refused to go into any details."

Nancy sat forward, cupping her chin in her hands. "Hmm," she said thoughtfully, "if you ask me, Dell, the person who kidnapped Walter probably talked him into breaking off the engagement."

"Why do you think that, Nancy?" Dell asked.

"Because the kidnapper is probably the same

person who wants to keep the Van Hoogstraten Collection from opening," Nancy declared. "And that person wants you to break up with Walter so you'll stay in your house and it won't become a museum."

"I'll bet you're right, Nancy," Bess chimed in. Looking at Dell, she added fervently, "You said Walter said he still loves you, so someone must have forced him to break things off. I just know it, Dell."

Dell brightened. "Do you really think so?" she asked, looking expectantly at all three girls.

Nancy smiled. "I really think so," she said.

Nancy cast her mind back to the conversation at S.O.I., when she had wondered whether Dell might be the person who wanted to jinx the museum. She had thought that Dell might be trying to manipulate Walter into moving into her New York house. But looking at Dell's hopeful eyes, Nancy couldn't believe that she would do such a thing to Walter, whom she obviously loved. And even if Dell was a really good liar, Nancy thought, how would kidnapping Walter and then letting him go get her what she wanted?

Nancy stood up. "I'm sure that the sooner I solve this case, the sooner you and Walter will patch things up."

Squaring her shoulders, Dell looked Nancy in the eye. "How can I help you, Nancy?" she asked.

"Do you have any old letters or papers of Julius's?" Nancy asked.

"Hmm," Dell said. "I've been sending things to storage in Boston this past month as I've gotten ready to move—mainly old family letters and stuff. But there's one box of legal documents I haven't dealt with yet. It's in a storeroom on the third floor. I'm not sure what you'll find in it, but let's hope for the best."

Dell led the three girls to a dusty room on the third floor of the house. In a corner was a box marked Old Family Documents in black marking pen.

"I'm beat, girls," Dell announced, stifling a yawn. "The stress of Walter's leaving has been too much for me. Do you mind if I go downstairs and rest? Let me know if you need anything else."

Nancy assured her they'd be fine and encouraged her to take a well-deserved break. After Dell had left, Nancy, George, and Bess began sorting through the old yellow documents. Some of them were leases and deeds that were no longer relevant. Others were old marriage licenses and birth certificates.

Scanning the documents, Nancy's heart sank with disappointment. Nothing in them suggested a clue to the case.

Bess and George rummaged around at the bottom of the box, making sure they hadn't missed anything important. "What's this?" Bess wondered, drawing out a thick official-looking document and handing it to Nancy.

Nancy frowned as she concentrated on the graceful script at the top of the page that read, "From the Estate of Julius Van Hoogstraten: His Personal Property as of May 10, 1915."

"This looks like a list of Julius's furniture and stuff after he died," Nancy said, reading the columns describing furniture, jewelry, and cars. She turned a page. "Oh, here's a list of his birds."

Nancy read down the list until her gaze fell upon the description of the crystal dove. "Listen to this, guys," she said, getting ready to quote from the document. " 'One finely fashioned crystal dove with a faint aquamarine hue. This unique object has a distinctive olive branch pattern carved upon its belly, suggesting Noah's dove. This object is an extremely valuable piece of crystal work. It has been in Julius Van Hoogstraten's possession since 1900.' "

"That's got to be the missing dove," George cut in. "Should we show this to Dell?"

"Definitely," Nancy said, "but first let's make sure there aren't more clues in any of these other documents."

After checking out the rest of the papers and finding nothing worthwhile, the girls put them away. Then they took the list of Julius's possessions downstairs to Dell, who was lying on the sofa in the sitting room reading a magazine.

Nancy showed her the document, then said, "One thing I don't get—why would this list say that Julius owned the dove since 1900? I mean, didn't he make all of his birds before he emigrated to America?"

"Nancy, you're right," Dell said, peering carefully at the list. "By 1900, when he supposedly first had this dove, Julius would have been running his railroad empire. He would have been way too busy at that point to do glasswork."

"Maybe this was a different dove," George reasoned. "Maybe Julius bought it in 1900, but the family no longer has it. It could have been sold off between 1915 and now."

"Do you remember whether the stolen dove had an olive design on its belly?" Bess asked Dell.

"I don't know," Dell said, frowning. "For as long as I can remember, the stolen dove just sat on the pedestal in the Aviary. I never noticed whether it had an olive branch design."

"So there's no way to tell whether the dove on this list is the stolen one," Nancy said.

Before anyone could reply, a key turned in the lock of the front door. Seconds later Alden walked into the sitting room.

"Bess!" he said happily as his gaze rested upon her. "You remembered our plans to take a carriage ride in the park?"

"I wouldn't forget an invitation like that," Bess told him, smiling.

Alden glanced at George and Nancy. "Why don't you guys join us? There's no reason you two should miss the fun." To Dell, he added, "And you're welcome to come, too, cousin."

"Thanks, Alden, but I think I'll stay here to try to chill out." Dell filled Alden in about Walter's reappearance.

"That is so weird, Dell," Alden said, looking troubled. "Don't let Walter talk you into calling off the police. They should still try to figure out what happened."

Dell glanced at the three girls. "When you girls were upstairs, I called Detective Phillips and told her that Walter had reappeared. They said that if Walter doesn't want to press charges, there's nothing they can do."

"We should tell them about the dove if we don't find it soon," Alden suggested.

"Let's give it another day," Dell said. "I don't want any negative publicity about the museum."

Half an hour later Nancy, Bess, George, and Alden were standing on Fifty-ninth Street on the border of Central Park. Elegantly dressed women strolled down nearby Fifth Avenue, while shoppers filed through the doorways of famous stores such as Tiffany's, Bergdorf Goodman, and F.A.O. Schwarz. The trees in Central Park swayed festively in a light breeze, their green leaves fluttering.

Alden approached a carriage driver standing by his huge dappled gray horse. "Can the four of us take a ride?" he asked.

"Certainly," the driver said. The man peered at the girls from under the brim of his cap. "Climb aboard, ladies. Jupiter and I will take you for a relaxing ride around the park." With a frisky toss of his head, Jupiter seemed eager to start. He pawed the ground impatiently as Alden paid the fee.

The man, whose gray hair matched that of his horse, climbed on to the driver's seat while Bess stepped into the open carriage. Grabbing a nearby handle, Nancy hoisted herself onto the outside step.

Just as she was about to swing herself into the carriage, Jupiter bolted forward. Nancy struggled to keep her balance on the step, hanging onto the flimsy handle as the horse and carriage careened down the street.

Out of the corner of her eye, Nancy saw Jupiter toss his head violently, yanking the reins out of the driver's hands. Barreling down the street behind the frenzied horse, the carriage suddenly leaped the curb.

Terrified pedestrians scattered as the carriage knocked down a street sign. The horse galloped across the sidewalk toward a stone wall.

Nancy held her breath as she hung from the side of the carriage. If Jupiter jumped the wall, the carriage would crash!

# 12

## Clued In

Jupiter slowed as the wall loomed in front of him. Out of the corner of her eye Nancy saw Alden racing alongside the carriage, gritting his teeth as he struggled to catch up.

The horse skittered away from the wall, and Alden reacted. He leaped up to grab the reins and tugged on them hard until the horse finally stopped.

"Whoa, boy," Alden said soothingly, patting the trembling creature. The horse snorted, scattering flecks of foam in the air.

Nancy jumped down, then helped Bess out of the coach. "What was that all about?" Bess asked, her body quivering with shock.

Before Nancy could answer, the driver climbed from his box to join Alden. With a trembling hand, he took the reins and said, "Thank you so much. I don't know what caused Jupiter here to bolt like that."

"You almost ran over me!" an angry woman shouted from a group of horrified onlookers. "I'll sue you for trauma."

"I'm so sorry, ma'am," the driver said. "Were you hurt?"

"No," she said, "but I could have been if this gentleman hadn't come along to stop your horse."

"What do you think happened?" Alden asked the driver.

The man shrugged. "Jupiter's young and recently trained. Maybe the traffic startled him."

Alden joined Nancy, Bess, and George. "Let's hire another carriage," he suggested.

"I'm game," Nancy said.

"Me, too," George said. "After all, the chances that there are two crazed horses in this park are pretty slim," she added wryly.

"Count me out," Bess declared. "No way am I getting into one of those things again."

"Oh, Bess, come on," Alden coaxed. "George is right. That kind of freaky accident isn't going to happen again to us." Squeezing her hand, he added, "I promise."

Bess sighed. "Well, okay," she said warily.

"Good," Alden pronounced. "Let's hire this guy

here." He pointed to a sober-looking chestnut horse nodding sleepily in the sunlight. "Something tells me he's had years of experience."

Ten minutes later Nancy, George, and Bess were happily riding through the park with Alden behind a completely unflappable carriage horse named Norm.

"I wonder what happened to make Jupiter so crazy?" Bess wondered as they plodded along. "Norm sure is different. His name kind of describes him."

"Must have been the traffic as the driver said," George guessed.

The carriage took a turn onto a leafy road where bicyclists and in-line skaters whizzed by. Nancy could no longer see any skyscrapers bordering the park.

"It's hard to believe we're even in New York," she said, leaning back comfortably in her seat.

"New York is really a group of neighborhoods," Alden said. "Each one has its own personality. When you live here, it doesn't seem like such a big, unfriendly place." He scowled suddenly and added, "Unless you've just had a valuable crystal dove stolen."

"So do you still suspect Richard Schoonover?" Nancy asked him.

"Yes!" Alden said passionately. "I'm sure Richard's guilty. He's always been envious of Julius's reputation, thanks to a family grudge that's been handed down through generations in his family."

"His ancestor Gustav Kinderhook must have

talked nonstop about how much he hated Julius," George said.

"No doubt about it," Alden said darkly.

"We know you suspect Mr. Schoonover," Bess said, edging closer to Alden. "But is there anyone else you think might be guilty?"

"Only Violet," Alden replied, "because she'd like to keep Dell in New York."

Nancy shot a curious look at Alden. "Why don't *you* want to live in the house?" she asked. "Then it could stay a private family home."

Alden grimaced. "No, thanks. The thought of living in an heirloom gives me the creeps. I like my loft down in Tribeca. It's got a modern style to it that's not stuffy like the house. And the neighborhood is younger—much hipper. I don't feel as if I'm living in the past."

"I don't know about you guys," Bess cut in, "but I'm ready for the Plaza. I mean, I trust Norm and all now, but I wouldn't mind a change of scene."

Alden gave her the thumbs-up sign, then shouted directions to the driver to take them back to Fifty-ninth Street. A few minutes later the foursome walked through the revolving doors of the Plaza Hotel.

"This hotel is so beautiful!" Bess gushed, looking around at the high ceilings, plush carpets, sumptuous marble fixtures, and potted palms swaying at the edge of the Palm Court, where tea was being served.

An orchestra at the back of the room struck up a tune.

"I could never get tired of this place," Bess added. "It kind of sums up glamorous modern New York City."

"New York has always been glittering and grand," Alden said as the maître d' in the Palm Court showed them to a table. "No matter whether it's the Gilded Age, when my great-grandfather lived, or the 1920s, the 1980s, or now."

George elbowed Bess and pointed to a large trolley filled with colorfully decorated pastries. "Wow!" Bess exclaimed. "Those things are awesome. Look at that mocha cake with the layers and swirls on the frosting. It's like the pastry equivalent of the Plaza."

Nancy laughed—and then stopped short as her gaze traveled across the magnificent room. At the entrance of the Palm Court—next to a group of grandly dressed ladies—was a familiar face. "Richard Schoonover," she said.

Nancy gasped. Dell was rushing over to him!

Dell touched Schoonover's shoulder. He whipped around, then smiled, shaking her hand vigorously.

The maître d' beckoned Schoonover and Dell to follow him to a table. But as he stepped farther into the room, Schoonover locked gazes with Nancy and stopped abruptly.

Schoonover grabbed Dell's arm, then did an

about-face. Without a backward glance, he escorted Dell through the hotel lobby and disappeared from Nancy's sight.

"Hey, guys," Nancy said to everyone at her table. "Did you see that? Richard Schoonover and Dell were going to sit down here, but when they saw me, they cut out."

"Let's follow them," George said, springing up from her chair.

"And sacrifice those great pastries?" Bess asked, stricken. "No way!"

"Then you stay here with Alden, Bess, while George and I go," Nancy suggested.

The two girls hurried through the room and out of the hotel. As they raced down the stairs to the sidewalk, they saw Dell slamming the door of a nearby cab.

"Let's take the next one," Nancy urged. She yanked open the door of a waiting cab and tumbled inside with George behind her. "Can you follow the taxi ahead of us waiting at the red light?" she asked the driver.

"No problem, lady," the driver said. His tires screeched as he pulled away from the curb just in time to catch up with Schoonover and Dell's cab before the light turned green.

Schoonover and Dell's cab wove through the midtown traffic in an effortless flash, missing vehicles by inches as the driver skillfully threaded his way downtown. No matter how fast the other cab went, Nancy and George's cab was behind it, like a watchful mother hen.

"Hey, this is kind of fun," George declared as they zoomed by the Empire State Building.

"I think so, too," Nancy said, her blue eyes fixed on Schoonover's cab. Soon the massive buildings gave way to a leafy square bordered by elegant nineteenth century brownstones. "We're heading into Greenwich Village," Nancy commented.

Minutes later the stately cast iron buildings of SoHo flashed by them, and Schoonover's cab took a left on to Spring Street.

"It's stopping at the Glass Slipper," George cried, pointing. "Quick—let's pull over behind them. Schoonover and Dell are getting out."

Nancy handed the cabbie the fare and a generous tip the moment he stopped the cab. Then she and George hopped out and rushed to the door of Schoonover's shop.

Nancy pushed on the door as Schoonover held it shut from the inside. "Please let us in!" she cried.

Shaking his head sternly, Schoonover tried to bolt the door. But before the lock slid across it, Nancy and George threw their weight against the door. It opened a crack.

"What is the meaning of this break-in?" Schoonover sputtered as Nancy and George pushed their way inside. "If you two don't leave these premises immediately, I'll be forced to call the police."

Dell blinked in surprise at Schoonover's threat as she observed the activity. "Don't be silly, Richard," she said. "You don't need to call the police on Nancy and George. They're trying to help me."

"How do I know that?" Schoonover snapped.

"Just take my word for it," Dell said. "You can trust Nancy and George with the information you were about to give me."

Schoonover peered haughtily at the girls from beneath his bushy white brows. "All right. But you girls had better not tell another living soul what I'm about to reveal."

"We won't," Nancy promised.

With his ice blue eyes flashing, Schoonover proclaimed, "Well, then, I saw it—the clue on the crystal bird!"

# 13

## A Ghostly Welcome

Dell looked at Schoonover as if he'd lost his mind. "What are you talking about, Richard?" she asked sharply.

"My memory has finally returned," he announced. "You see, before I was hit on the head, I'd examined the crystal dove and noticed an olive branch design on its belly. The knock on my head drove away that memory until now."

"You mean the knock on your head gave you amnesia?" George asked.

"Sort of," Schoonover replied. "I remembered most things, like my name and the job I was doing for Delphinia. I just forgot what had happened immediately before I was struck. But I remember everything now, and the olive pattern on the dove was unmistakable."

Nancy, George, and Dell exchanged glances. "Julius's list," Nancy mouthed to them.

"I suppose you're all wondering what's so special about that olive branch design," Schoonover cut in. "Well, let me tell you."

Dell drew up a nearby chair and sat down, while Nancy and George leaned against the counter. Warming to his story, Schoonover said, "You might be aware that one of my ancestors was Gustav Kinderhook. Now, Gustav happened to be Julius Van Hoogstraten's mentor in Holland—the old country. Julius learned glassblowing and crystal making from Gustav, who was renowned for his artistic talent and his teaching skills."

Clearing his throat, Schoonover continued, "Gustav always signed his crystal work by carving an olive branch into the glass. That beautiful dove was his very first work in crystal. I believe he meant it to be Noah's dove that was sent out from the ark. Anyway, Gustav was inspired to carve that design into all his later work. It was his special mark to show that he'd created the piece."

"What a lovely idea!" Dell exclaimed.

Schoonover looked at her fiercely. "Don't you understand, Delphinia? The crystal dove in your house that Julius claimed to have made was really by Gustav. Julius was a fraud!"

"Julius—a fraud?" Dell echoed, paling. "I can't believe it."

"Well, you'd better believe it," Schoonover declared, "because I have proof. The olive pattern is described in Gustav's diary. I wanted to show you the diary and tell you that I remembered the olive branch on Julius's dove before I was knocked out."

"So if you didn't steal the dove, Richard, then who did?" Dell asked him.

"I don't know who took it," he replied, "but I do know why. The thief wants to keep the world from discovering the olive pattern. This person is desperate to keep the collection from opening because if enough experts like myself saw it, someone would eventually figure out that the birds were created by Gustav."

"And you invited me to the Plaza to tell me all this?" Dell asked. "Why not a phone call?"

"Because I wanted you to see Gustav's diary in case you didn't believe me," Schoonover replied. "I had an appointment on Fifty-ninth Street earlier in the afternoon, and I thought that the Plaza would be a convenient and pleasant place to discuss this matter. I didn't want anyone but you to know my suspicions, Delphinia. I feel that you are discreet."

Scowling at Nancy and George, he added, "But when I saw your group, I hurried away. I don't want everyone in the world to know about my discovery. The person who hit me on the head means business.

I don't want to tip off anyone else about what I know."

"Don't worry, Mr. Schoonover. George and I won't tell anyone," Nancy assured him.

"I certainly hope not," Schoonover said curtly.

"I've been thinking," Dell said. "Maybe there was some mistake about the dove. Maybe Julius had always given Gustav credit for it, but later Julius's descendants assumed that it had been made by Julius. Maybe it was an honest mistake."

Schoonover looked at her as if he were about to explode. Drawing himself up to his full height, which was considerably less than that of Nancy, George, or Dell, he said, "Delphinia! I promise you—Julius never gave Gustav any credit, and the glasswork in the house is all Gustav's. There is no doubt."

"All the birds are Gustav's?" Dell asked in a shocked tone. "How do you know?"

"Do they all have the olive pattern on them?" Nancy asked.

"I don't believe Gustav's regular glasswork had that pattern," Schoonover answered. "Just his crystal. Still, I know I am right. Julius was a fraud. His entire glass collection was done by Gustav."

"But if Gustav's regular glasswork didn't have that pattern, then how can you prove he made Julius's birds?" George asked.

"There were special colors Gustav liked to use—deep purples and magentas that bordered on ruby. Julius's birds all have colors that Gustav favored," Schoonover explained. "Also, Julius's parrot has only one wing, just like Gustav's pet parrot, which he often used as a model. And the design of Julius's swallowtails has a delicacy that only Gustav could produce. I assure you, young lady, I am right," Schoonover said stubbornly, "although I suppose I can't absolutely prove my case."

Nancy's blue eyes sparkled. "The letters on the train!" she exclaimed. "I bet the stolen letters mention that Gustav made the birds. The person probably took the letters so no one would find out."

Briefly, Nancy filled in Dell and Schoonover about the missing documents in the train panel.

"If only we could find those letters, we might have proof that Julius was a fake," Schoonover remarked.

"There's a good chance the person who took the letters destroyed them so that no one would find out about Julius," Nancy pointed out. She turned to Dell and asked, "Are you sure you sent all of Julius's letters to Boston? If there are any left in your house, we might find one that mentions that Gustav made the birds."

Dell shook her head. "I'm sure I sent them all, Nancy. I guess I could arrange to get them back, but that might take weeks."

A moment of troubled silence filled the room while everyone tried to decide what to do next.

"Wait!" Dell exclaimed, shooting up from her chair. Her bright green eyes filled with excitement as she gazed at Nancy. "Fern Hill! I bet there are a bunch of letters there."

"Fern Hill?" Nancy asked "What's that?"

"Julius had a summer cabin at Birch Mountain Lake in the Adirondacks. Well, it wasn't exactly a cabin," Dell added with a wry chuckle. "It was more like a huge luxurious lakeside palace made to look rustic out of logs and birchbark. The main house has about seven fireplaces with a moose head hanging over each one, Persian rugs on the floor, and valuable Audubon prints on the walls. The place has canoes, a private lakeside dock, and a tennis court. There's even a stone turret built for Julius's eccentric brother to stay in when he visited. Lots of wealthy people during the Gilded Age had these amazing retreats in the Adirondacks, and I think Fern Hill was one of the grandest."

"It sounds really cool," George said. "I'm amazed that it's stayed in your family all these years."

"Julius's houses are unique and so full of family atmosphere that none of his descendants has wanted to give them up," Dell explained. "We did sell his Newport, Rhode Island, cottage back in the sixties—'cottage' meaning a twenty-five–room mansion on

121

the beach. The upkeep got to be too expensive. But some of us—like Aunt Violet—still use Fern Hill."

"And you think there's a chance we'd find some letters there?" Nancy pressed.

Dell chewed her lip, then said, "There's a chance. The place has fallen into disrepair, but if any old papers or letters were ever there, they've probably remained untouched. I mean, no one ever does much with the place to change it. Every now and then we get it cleaned, and we have a handyman make necessary repairs so the roof won't leak. But the last time I was there, I noticed medicines in the bathroom left over from the 1940s."

"Good gracious!" Mr. Schoonover exclaimed. "The place is a relic."

"But you said your aunt Violet goes there sometimes?" Nancy asked Dell.

"She's the only person I know who visits there regularly," Dell answered. "She loves the lake, and she doesn't mind the creaky old house. No one is there now, though—you're welcome to camp in one of the rooms."

Nancy turned to George. "How soon can you get packed for a trip to the Adirondacks?"

"In seconds," George answered cheerfully.

"We'll tell Bess she's only allowed to bring one suitcase," Nancy declared. A sudden memory tugged at Nancy's mind. "You know what? Aunt Eloise has a summer place in the Adirondacks, and I think it's near Birch Mountain Lake. We might be more comfortable staying there if it's okay with Aunt Eloise."

"So what are we waiting for?" George asked, heading for the door. "Let's go back to Eloise's and book the next flight to the Adirondacks."

Dell looked Nancy and George in the eye. "If you can prove that Julius was a fraud," she said, "I'll cancel our plans to open his collection. Unlike him, I would never lie to the public." To Schoonover, she added, "Don't worry, Richard. If it turns out you're right, I'll be sure to credit Gustav Kinderhook as the real artist—publically."

"If you do that, Dell," Nancy said, "the person who's causing all the weird stuff around your house will probably stop—even if we never find out who he or she is."

"That makes sense," George said, "because if everyone learns that Julius's collection is really Gustav's, the bad guy won't have a reason to keep it from opening. Everyone will already know the worst."

"And life at your house will return to normal, Delphinia," Schoonover said confidently.

"Still, I'd like to know who the bad guy is," Nancy said to George as they walked out the door.

"This view is awesome," Bess said as she looked out the window of the small chartered plane.

123

"The lakes below us are dazzling in the early evening light," Aunt Eloise agreed, from the seat beside Bess. Behind them, Nancy and George talked about the case so far.

"It's too bad Dell couldn't come with us on this adventure," George said. "But it was really generous of her to charter this airplane for us."

"It sure was," Nancy agreed. "If we'd taken a regular flight, we wouldn't have arrived until way after dark. We couldn't have looked for any letters till tomorrow, since Fern Hill doesn't have electricity."

"We're already pushing it with the time," Aunt Eloise said, craning her neck to look back at Nancy and George. "It's six-thirty now. After landing at the airport and getting a cab, we probably won't be at my cabin till almost eight. At least it's June, and the sun sets late."

"It's lucky that your cabin is also on Birch Mountain Lake," George remarked to Aunt Eloise. "What a coincidence."

"It's not a total coincidence," Aunt Eloise told them. "Dell and I first met each other because Fern Hill was across the lake from my cabin. I met her one day years ago at a local arts fund-raiser."

"So why couldn't Dell come with us?" Bess asked, glancing back at Nancy and George.

"She wanted to stay in town to try to patch things up with Walter," Nancy said. "After he broke off their engagement, he moved to a hotel while he does some research at the Bronx Zoo."

The gentle whirring of the engines made Nancy sleepy, and after several minutes of silence, she leaned her head against the window and fell sound asleep.

True to Eloise Drew's prediction, the cab pulled into her unpaved driveway at exactly three minutes before eight. As everyone took bags out of the trunk, Aunt Eloise pointed to a green station wagon parked near her cabin and said, "I always leave my car here and take cabs to and from the airport. But now that we've arrived, we can drive wherever we want."

"Or boat wherever we want," George said, eyeing the blue lake spread in front of the house. The water beckoned magically in the hazy dusk.

"I'd like to go over to Fern Hill right now," Nancy said, tempted by the sight of a canoe resting on the porch of her aunt's cabin. "There's still some light, and I really want to start my search."

Aunt Eloise frowned. "Don't you think it's a little late, Nancy? We haven't had dinner yet, and I thought I'd take us out to this pizza joint in the village of Birch Mountain, five miles away. Plus, there are big clouds hovering on the horizon."

Biting her lip, Nancy thought about her aunt's advice. But she felt in a rush to look for the letters. "It's only a matter of time before this person realizes there might be letters up here," she reasoned. "We might already be too late. Whether I go now or tomorrow could make a big difference."

Aunt Eloise sighed. "The only boat I have is this canoe, and it gets tippy with more than one person in it. I don't feel right about your going over there alone, Nancy."

Nancy smiled. "I'll be fine, Aunt Eloise, really."

Twenty minutes later Nancy was paddling the canoe through the still, dark water of Birch Mountain Lake. The sun had slipped behind an elephant-shaped hill on the horizon, and the sky was deepening to a hazy purple. Trying her best to paddle silently, Nancy winced every time the oar made an unexpected splashing noise. In the silence around her, it sounded deafening.

Soon a huge dilapidated cabin loomed in front of her—Fern Hill, Nancy guessed from Dell's description. As the canoe coasted up on the rocky shore, Nancy started.

In the failing light a shadow hovered on the porch of the house. Then the figure slipped inside.

126

# 14

## Terror on the Lake

Nancy froze. Dell had told her that the place would be empty.

Nancy landed the canoe on the rocky shore and stepped out. After pulling it out of the water, Nancy crept toward the house on a woodland path, her sneakers silent on a carpet of pine needles.

As she moved closer, Nancy saw that Dell was right—the house could use some attention. Made of logs, with moss-covered birch railings circling its porch, it had definitely passed its prime. Still, the house must have been wonderful in its day, Nancy thought, with its turrets and stained glass windows.

A sudden breeze blew up as Nancy cautiously climbed the steps to the porch. Rocking chairs creaked eerily in the wind, as if a family of ghosts were outside to greet her. A chill snaked down her neck as she glanced around. Not a soul was there.

A soft glow suddenly filled the downstairs windows, and Nancy started. With her heart hammering away, she peeked through a window.

A kerosene lamp glimmered on a dining room table, providing a dim light. Nancy could see a jumble of artifacts decorating an enormous lodgelike room. Mounted moose heads, with old-fashioned hats stuck on their antlers, presided over two enormous stone fireplaces at opposite ends of the room. Bearskin rugs with snarling jaws took up space on the pine floor along with worn oriental rugs. Boxes of games and puzzles that looked as if they hadn't been played in years gathered dust on an oak table. Through a doorway on the left, Nancy could see part of an old-fashioned sink and some cabinets—the kitchen, she reasoned.

A shadow passed by the window. Nancy tensed. It was Violet, and she was carrying a cardboard box!

Nancy stepped backward in surprise. A board creaked loudly under her feet. Violet dropped the box, her startled eyes flying toward the window.

"Who's there?" Violet said.

For a moment Nancy remained completely still, thinking of what to do. If she ran away, she'd lose her

128

chance to see what was inside the box. What if Julius's letters were there and Violet was about to destroy them?

But if she tried to sneak around the place, Violet would surely find her, with all the creaky floorboards. Then Violet—if she was guilty—would be in an even bigger hurry to get rid of Julius's letters.

Nancy decided that her best bet was to make up a story explaining why she was there and hope that Violet would swallow it.

"Who's there?" Violet repeated, her voice shaking. "I may not have a telephone, but I have a flare that will bring the police if I set it off."

"I'm sorry to bother you," Nancy said, "but I'm lost."

Violet stepped outside. The sky was now completely dark, and she squinted in Nancy's direction.

Nancy moved into the slice of light near the doorway. "Violet? It's Nancy Drew."

"Nancy!" Violet exclaimed. "Goodness me! Don't we end up in the oddest places together? What are you doing at Fern Hill? You say you're lost?"

"Yes," Nancy replied. "I'm staying at my aunt Eloise's cabin on the other side of the lake. I was out canoeing, but then it got dark and now I can't find my way back."

"What a coincidence that we both decided to travel to the Adirondacks today," Violet said, her lavender hair puffing out from under a golf cap. "But we did have some rough times this past week, what with all those strange things going on at the house. I simply couldn't handle it a moment longer, and I see that you couldn't, either. Are your two nice friends with you?"

"We're all staying at my aunt's cabin," Nancy replied.

"But you were out on the lake alone," Violet scolded, shaking a skinny finger at Nancy. "What if your canoe had capsized? No one would hear from you again."

"I'm a good swimmer," Nancy told her.

"Ah, but this lake can be deadly," Violet pronounced. "It's not to be trusted. Would you like to rest up inside before you start home? It would be lovely to chat with you for a while, Nancy."

Nancy followed Violet inside. Shooting a glance at the box Violet had been holding, Nancy saw that it was full of old letters.

A thrill went through her. But when Violet sat down in a nearby chair, Nancy's excitement turned to frustration. How can I sneak a look at the letters with Violet here? she wondered.

"Uh, Violet," Nancy said, pulling up the zipper of her sweatshirt, "I'm a little cold from being out on the lake for so long. Could I have a cup of tea, please?"

Violet shot up from her chair. "Where are my manners?" she muttered. "Of course you may have some tea, my dear. Excuse me."

The moment Violet turned her back, Nancy kneeled down by the cardboard box. She slipped off her sweatshirt and got to work. On the top of the box were letters addressed to Van Hoogstratens she hadn't heard of. But as she dug deeper, she found a letter addressed to Julius Van Hoogstraten, with Gustav Kinderhook's return address.

With mounting excitement, Nancy opened the letter. "Dear Julius," she read, "It's lucky for me that I'm fluent in English because I wouldn't want my wife and daughter to look over my shoulder as I write and know my distressing news.

"I have discovered that you are passing off my glasswork as your own. A fellow Dutch glassworker, Hans Guilder, saw your collection when he attended a party at your house as an escort to a young lady you'd invited. Maybe you did not realize that Hans was a colleague familiar with my work. If you had, you probably would not have allowed him inside.

"Hans was interested to learn that you'd created a display of glass birds when you'd lived in Holland. But the moment he saw them he was suspicious because they are so distinctly my own style. And when he saw my olive branch upon the crystal dove, he was

131

convinced of your treachery. He immediately told me about your terrible deed.

"Yes, Julius, you *did* buy the birds from me before you went to America because you had always admired them, but you did not buy the right to tell the world that you had made them. I can't believe that you—my former pupil and employee—would do such a thing. What has the world come to when you betray an old teacher such as myself?

"I am highly displeased. I am planning to correct your act of piracy by letting the world know that I am the true creator of your beautiful ornithological display. Mark my words, Julius, you will be shamed before everyone. Sincerely, Gustav Kinderhook."

Nancy looked up to make sure that Violet wasn't there. Sure enough, she was still bustling around in the kitchen, slamming cabinet doors and singing to herself.

Nancy folded the letter and stuffed it in the pocket of her sweatshirt lying on the floor. Then she dug back into the box. Even if I don't find anything else, Nancy thought, this letter proves that the Van Hoogstraten Collection is a fake.

As she searched in the box, Nancy felt a pang of sadness as she thought about the Van Hoogstraten family. They had believed their ancestor had this great artistic talent, when all he had really created was a terrible deception. He must have been desperate to be known for something other than his wealth, Nancy thought.

Nancy's gaze focused on a letter with familiar handwriting near the bottom of the box. This one was also addressed to Julius with Gustav's return address. Nancy opened the envelope.

"Dear Julius," she read, "I want to thank you for the $10,000 that you sent me to buy my silence. Rest assured that I will tell no one I am the true creator of your glass bird collection.

"I took your money reluctantly. If the money had been for me, I would have reported your fraud and not accepted the payment, but I desperately need it to pay my sick daughter's medical expenses. She has been very ill, but the money can buy her an expensive new treatment. There is finally hope for her. I must be grateful for that, even though I hate myself for participating in your rotten scheme.

"I trust this will be the last of our letters. Sincerely, Gustav Kinderhook."

As Nancy's eyes scanned the last line, she paused. Someone was behind her—she could tell. Violet with my tea? she wondered.

A sharp blow cracked down on her head, and Nancy crumpled to the floor, too stunned to cry out. As she lay on the floor helplessly, she could feel her legs being lifted up and her body hauled toward the open front door.

From the kitchen Violet's cheerful voice rang out, "Nancy, dear, do you take cream and sugar in your tea?"

Nancy thought about screaming for help. But even if she could muster up the strength, what good would it do? she wondered. Violet was no match for this person, and anyway the lodge had no phone. The attacker seemed pretty strong, and if Violet tried to get in the way, she might end up hurt, too.

Nancy closed her eyes, pretending to be unconscious. After all, she reasoned, she was too weak to fight, and she might as well gather her strength. She had a feeling she would need it later.

The person stopped at the porch stairs and lifted Nancy up. A low grunt made Nancy realize that her attacker was a man.

Hoisting her onto his back, the man headed toward the lake, his footsteps thumping on the path. Nancy's head hung below his shoulders, and in the dark, she had no way of telling who he was.

A bolt of lightning ripped through the sky, but all Nancy could see was the bottom of a pair of blue jeans tucked into sturdy hiking boots.

Thunder blasted through the air. Seconds later Nancy saw her aunt's canoe below her on the shore. The person laid Nancy down inside it. Then he pushed the canoe into the dark water and climbed inside.

Sitting in the back, he began to paddle. The canoe made hardly a sound as it glided over the calm lake water.

Slowly Nancy felt her strength returning. Deciding that she could fight back if she had to, Nancy sneaked a glance at the person above her.

# 15

## Birds of a Feather

A chill went through Nancy as lightning illuminated the steely eyes of Alden Guest.

The lightning died, and a thunderclap instantly followed. The skies opened, and a torrential rain swept over the lake, lashing the water brutally. But Nancy could still see Alden, staring ahead as he rowed with firm, swift strokes.

Alden's eyes flickered toward Nancy as he switched his paddle to the other side of the canoe.

His gaze locked with hers. "So you're awake, Nancy," he snarled. "I'll have to do a better job on you this time." He raised his oar to strike her as she lay at the bottom of the canoe.

Nancy didn't wait another second. As lightning

flashed through the sky again, she raised her leg and karate kicked Alden in the chest.

Knocked off balance by Nancy's attack, Alden dropped the paddle in the water as his arms flailed in the air. The canoe rocked wildly back and forth, and Nancy remembered Aunt Eloise's warning that it could carry only one person safely.

More lightning lit up the sky as they struggled to right the canoe. But it was no use. Seconds later the canoe tipped over, plunging them into the water.

Sheets of rain pounded the canoe. Nancy held onto it as she yelled for Alden. "We've got to get off the lake!" she cried. "The lightning."

Alden popped up on the other side of the canoe. "Not until I've taken care of you," he cried, then disappeared below it.

He's going to pull me under the water, Nancy thought. She began to swim, taking strong even strokes as she forced herself to stay calm. But which way is the closest shore? she wondered, her eyes struggling to penetrate the thick darkness.

Another streak of lightning lit up the lake for what seemed like an eternity, and Nancy saw the shore about fifty feet away.

Something splashed behind her. Nancy shot a look over her shoulder before the lightning died. Adrenaline shot down her spine. Alden was gaining on her.

Nancy plunged ahead, expecting Alden to grab

her ankle at any second. Thunder echoed across the lake as Nancy swam. Her arm muscles ached with the strain of swimming, and she choked down waves that slammed into her whenever she gasped for air. But no matter how hard it was to swim in the middle of the storm, she forced herself to press on.

I've got to swim faster, she told herself. I can't let him catch me.

A blinding flash and then a blast like an explosion ripped apart the air. Nancy whirled around. Flames engulfed a tree on a small island behind her. Lightning had struck it, she realized. She could be next— or Alden. But where was he?

A dark form rose up on her left. Nancy put her face back in the water and pressed on, her arms moving like knives as they sliced through the lake. She couldn't think about how tired she was. She had to keep moving.

Nancy felt something gripping her legs. Alden! she thought, with a stab of fear. But no—it was something soft and slimy, slick with algae. No matter how hard she tried to escape from its clutches, it wouldn't let her go.

Nancy reached into the water and tugged at the weeds, trying to free her legs. But she was completely tangled. A shudder ran through her—she felt as if an octopus or a lake monster had snagged her from the deep.

Nancy jerked at the stems in frustration. She tried to move again, but it was as if she were in a nightmare. No matter how hard she struggled, her legs wouldn't move.

Nancy heard a splash about five feet away. Alden would be on her in seconds.

Nancy yanked desperately at the weeds that bound her legs, but they were too tough. She swiveled toward Alden, getting ready for a fight.

Alden suddenly started thrashing. "I'm stuck!" he sputtered, his voice panicked.

Summoning all her energy, Nancy yanked the weeds once more. Relief flooded through her as the stems snapped. Finally she was free.

Skimming the surface of the water to avoid the weeds, Nancy shot toward shore. As she dragged herself from the chilly water, she scanned the area of the lake where she had last seen Alden.

Nancy started. Alden was five feet behind her, rising from the water on the rocky shore.

The rain poured over them as Alden held up a knife. "I had my penknife in my pocket," he explained. "Those weeds couldn't keep me down for long. Surprised, aren't you, Nancy?"

He stooped to pick up a rock. With that in one hand and his penknife in the other, he marched toward Nancy.

"You think you can escape from me, Nancy?" he

growled as lightning flared through the sky. "I must admit you were a challenge for a while, but now I've finally got you." He laughed, eyeing Nancy pitilessly.

"You don't have me yet, Alden," Nancy countered, trying to edge around him.

"I'll knock you out with this stone and throw you in the lake, and no one will ever suspect me," Alden declared. "Eloise will think you drowned when your canoe capsized in the storm."

For a split second Alden stared at her, his face a mask of hatred as more lightning glowed. Then he rushed her, holding up the stone. But Nancy was quicker. In two quick karate moves, she kicked the stone and the penknife from his hands. Shocked, Alden stepped back.

Nancy didn't give him a moment to relax. With one more kick in the chest, she knocked him to the ground.

"Hey, Nancy!" George's voice rang out from the porch of Fern Hill as a flashlight glimmered. "Guys, I think she's down there. I see a shadow by the lake."

"I'm here," Nancy yelled back, "with Alden."

"Alden?" she heard Bess gasp.

"Nancy, be careful. We're coming," Aunt Eloise cried. "The sheriff is with us."

"The sheriff?" Alden moaned as he lay on the ground. Leaning on his elbows, he gazed despondently at the group dashing down the path from Fern Hill. "Then it's all over for me."

Seconds later the sheriff appeared—a stout, middle-aged man—followed by Bess, George, and Eloise Drew.

The sheriff went straight to Alden, pulled his arms behind his back, and clamped a pair of handcuffs on his wrists. "The moment I stepped onto the porch of Fern Hill," he said, "I saw you attacking this young lady—before George alerted everyone that she was here. That bolt of lightning lit you up. Young man, I'm arresting you for assault at the very least." Looking at Nancy, he added, "I'm impressed by your self-defense skills. Those were some karate kicks."

"Thanks," Nancy said, smiling. To Aunt Eloise, George, and Bess, she added, "So how did you guys know that I was in danger here? I mean, you actually brought the sheriff."

"I can explain everything," the sheriff said. "Eloise called me the moment the storm started, because she was worried that you were out on the lake. Since my police station isn't far from her house, I picked up Eloise, George, and Bess on my way to Fern Hill. I thought there was a good chance you'd taken refuge here, and I wanted to check it out before searching the lake. I knew there was no phone here, so you wouldn't be able to call your aunt."

"Oh, Nancy, I'm so glad you're okay," Aunt Eloise said, hugging her. "My goodness, you're completely drenched. Let's get you back to the cabin. Violet has made a roaring fire."

A few minutes later Violet handed Nancy a cup of tea and a dry towel. "Stand here by the fire, dear. You'll be warm in no time. Of course, you could borrow some of Julius's second wife's clothes," Violet added doubtfully. "They've been gathering dust in her closet all these years. In fact, I was just cleaning out that closet when you first arrived."

"Don't worry, Violet," Nancy said, setting her teacup on a table while she dried her hair by the fire, "my clothes will dry out soon, thanks to your great fire."

"What a shocking thing you've done, Alden," Violet declared, glaring at him as he stood inside the lodge with the sheriff. "You've wounded our family pride."

"Time to get going," the sheriff said. "I've got to get this guy locked up. It's late."

"No, wait, please," Nancy said, putting down her towel. "Would you mind if we ask him a few questions first?"

The sheriff shrugged. "Fine by me," he said.

Facing Alden, who looked forlorn and bedraggled in his wet clothes, Nancy said, "I assume you took the papers that were in Julius's secret panel on the train, right?"

Alden's eyes flickered with surprise. "You knew about those letters? I discovered the truth about Julius's collection by reading them. A little while before I met you girls on the train, I found the secret panel by accident. I read Julius's letters, and—I was horrified." He glanced pitifully around the room. "I was so disappointed," he went on. "I'd always respected Julius so much. He was a role model and then—this happened."

"What else did the letters say?" Nancy asked.

"In one of them, Julius admitted to paying two art experts to claim that the glass birds had been made by him," Alden replied. "In another letter, he admits that he paid off Gustav. Then Julius banned all other glass experts from the house to protect his secret."

"I feel bad for you, Alden," Violet said, shaking her head. "You must have been shocked to discover that Julius was not the man we'd thought he was. More than anyone in our family, you looked up to him. But how could you stoop so low as to attack people? That dishonors our family more than anything Julius ever did."

Alden looked at her, his eyes filled with despair. "I'm sorry, Aunt Violet. I know I was wrong. But I had to protect Julius's memory at all costs. I knew that sooner or later his lie would be discovered if the collection became public."

"So you wrote all those threatening notes," Nancy prompted, crossing her arms, "and you made the chandelier fall, and you attacked Mr. Schoonover and stole the crystal bird."

"Yes," Alden said. "I had to hide the dove because of the olive pattern. Any expert would have known that Gustav had made it. It's in a desk drawer in my loft, by the way."

"Why did you have to kidnap Walter and make him break up with Dell?" Bess asked. "What you did to them was awful."

"I did that so Dell would stay in the house and our collection would remain private," Alden replied. "I told Walter that I would harm Dell if he didn't break up with her. He never realized who I was because I knocked him unconscious on a deserted path in my neighborhood. Earlier that day I'd overheard him on the phone, making an appointment to visit a colleague who lives near me. I waylaid Walter near my building, and once we got into my loft, I blindfolded him."

Bess shook her head, looking thoroughly disgusted.

"That morning I overheard Nancy offer to investigate the case," Alden went on. "Dell didn't realize that I was in the house, but I was hiding in a closet with the crystal dove in my briefcase. I couldn't close the door all the way. I had to wait for the foyer to empty out before I left."

"I assume you pushed Nancy off the bridge?" George asked.

Alden nodded. "Nancy was too good a detective. I knew she'd find out about me sooner or later."

"You were pushed off a bridge, Nancy?" Aunt Eloise asked, horrified. "Why didn't you tell me any of this?"

Nancy smiled. "I didn't want to worry you, Aunt Eloise." To Alden she said, "What about the carriage horse? Did you do something to spook him so I'd fall and get trampled?"

"I had a little spur in my pocket," Alden explained, "and it seemed like a perfect opportunity to injure you. But I rescued you guys at the last moment when I realized that Bess might get hurt, too."

Bess rolled her eyes. Nancy added, "And I guess you tripped the circuit breakers on the train."

"When I first read Julius's letters, Aunt Violet was asleep in one of his armchairs," Alden said. "She started to wake up, and I put them back because I didn't want her to see me take them. I didn't even want her to see the secret panel because she'd be curious to know what was in it. But I couldn't get her to leave the coach. I tripped the breakers so she wouldn't see me swipe the letters. But the lights came back on before I could finish the job, and I had to come back that night when everyone was asleep."

"You see, my dear," Violet said, winking at Nancy,

"I really was sleepwalking. I could tell that you didn't believe me at the time."

"What a gorgeous day!" Bess exclaimed. She and Nancy were standing by the lake in front of Aunt Eloise's cabin the following afternoon. The three girls were taking turns waterskiing, and it was George's turn now.

"A great day for relaxing after finishing up a case," Nancy added.

"It's hard to believe that Alden would commit those crimes just to protect Julius's reputation," Bess commented, shaking her head.

George waterskied toward shore as Aunt Eloise cut the engine of the motorboat she had borrowed. "Your turn now, Bess!" George yelled as she waded toward them.

An old Cadillac with fins pulled into the driveway. A moment later Dell and Walter climbed out and waved to Aunt Eloise and the girls, who were walking toward them from the lake.

"What a wonderful surprise!" Aunt Eloise said, throwing her arms around Dell and Walter. Stepping back, she looked at them fondly and added, "When I called you last night to give you the news about Alden, you didn't give me any idea that you were coming here today."

"Well, we have an even better surprise for you,"

Walter said, beaming. "Guess what? We're re-engaged!"

"That's awesome!" George exclaimed.

"I knew things would work out for you guys," Nancy said, smiling. "Congratulations."

"It was destiny," Bess pronounced, her blue eyes sparkling.

Everyone gathered on the porch, where a pitcher of iced tea was waiting. After Eloise had poured a glass for everyone, Dell explained, "Walter and I flew up here this morning to surprise you with the news. We're staying at Fern Hill for a few days with Violet. That's her car," she added, pointing at the Cadillac.

"How is Violet doing?" Nancy asked. "I hope she wasn't too upset by everything that happened last night."

"She's a real trooper," Dell said. "I talked to her and other Van Hoogstraten relatives, and everyone's sad to learn that Julius was so dishonest. We decided to sell his mansion and all the furniture, which I'm kind of relieved about. The house had become a burden. Now I can finally lead a normal life. By the way, the bird collection is going to a museum, with Gustav named as the artist."

"I hope you'll keep Fern Hill," Aunt Eloise said. "It's such a fixture around here."

"My relatives and I have decided to fix it up so we can take turns enjoying it," Dell told her.

"What about Richard Schoonover?" Nancy asked. "Does he know what happened?"

"I called Richard this morning to let him know that Gustav has finally been recognized as the true artist of the birds," Dell said. She looked gratefully at Nancy and added, "And I'd like to recognize you, Nancy Drew, as the true artist of mystery solving. Thank you so much for all your brilliant work. Without you, Walter and I wouldn't be together."

Walter and Dell grinned affectionately at each other, while Aunt Eloise raised her iced tea glass in a toast and said, "To Gustav, the true artist of the birds. And to Nancy, the true artist of mystery solving. Three cheers."

# *American* S·I·S·T·E·R·S

Join different sets of sisters as they embark on the varied, sometimes dangerous, always exciting journeys across America's landscape!

### West Along the Wagon Road, 1852

### A *Titanic* Journey Across the Sea, 1912

### Voyage to a Free Land, 1630

### Adventure on the Wilderness Road, 1775

### Crossing the Colorado Rockies, 1864

### Down the Rio Grande, 1829

### Horseback on the Boston Post Road, 1704

### Exploring the Chicago World's Fair, 1893

## by Laurie Lawlor

A MINSTREL® BOOK

Published by Pocket Books

2200-04